I0692373

DULAT ISSABEKOV

TURMOIL

NOVEL

London

2022

Published by Hertfordshire Press Ltd © 2022
e-mail: publisher@hertfordshirepress.com
www.hertfordshirepress.com

TURMOIL

Novel by DULAT ISSABEKOV

English

Translated from Russian by Timur Akhmedjanov
Edited by Gareth Stamp
Typeset Alexandra Rey

*British Library Catalogue in Publication Data
A catalogue record for this book is available from the British Library
Library of Congress in Publication Data
A catalogue record for this book has been requested*

ISBN: 978-1-913356-56-9

TURMOIL

NOVEL

PART ONE

...She was not yet eighteen years old, and life always seemed kind, fabulously beautiful and at any moment, as long as you can think of it, it can give you everything good and joyful that is in the world! Their family was the most famous in the district, and her parents believed that their daughter should not limit her education to the regular school curriculum, like many of her peers. They decided that she needed extra classes in history, music, and science. Bagila didn't resist this, especially since her teachers in school tirelessly praised her knowledge.

After leaving school, her father carved out a few days vacation, and personally took his daughter to Almaty.

Bagila rarely saw her father, Karatai. He left early, showed up at the door at midnight. He didn't talk to the kids very often. Even when he arrived at twelve o'clock, he immediately sat down and went on to his phone, as if people were only waiting for his call at night, he would begin to give instructions, sharply explain things, scolding... Bagila lay in her room and listened to what, and how her father said things, and was sincerely surprised. When does he rest? Sometimes she felt sorry for her father to the point of tears, especially when, through the crack of a half-closed door, she saw how he, having quarrelled with some unknown person, threw down the phone and with trembling hands, accepted a crystal glass from her mother, with Valocordin, cloudy white in the water. He calmed down slowly, sat in his armchair, ruffled and then closed his eyes, like a sick bird. And having calmed down, he grabbed the phone and asked for an apartment of the director of some distant state farm; the clock at that minute was already counting the first hour of the new day.

And so, she would fall asleep under the official conversations of her father.

She studied in the first shift. In the morning, in the beginning of the 7th, Bagila found out that her father's bed was empty, and the unfinished tea in his cup was barely warm... As if feeling guilty in front of his daughter, her father would often send a car that took her to school.

All this was familiar, normal, she did not even allow the thought that life could be different. Only with age, or rather, in her most recent years, Bagila began to seriously understand that her father's work was hellishly hard, that he worked with wear and tear, not thinking about himself, she understood that their family wealth, parental generosity, unchanged in relation to her, are all connected with her father, who always, as far as she could remember, did not know rest, day or night.

When they settled into a soft compartment of the branded "Kazakhstan" train, a lean, tall young man of about thirty years entered with them, he had a huge armful of newspapers and magazines, as if he had bought the entire contents of the kiosk standing on the platform. It seemed to her that he greeted them coldly, deliberately. Bagila gave a short nod in response and again began to look out the window at the platform with a smile, where her mother, brother, two sisters and several friends were standing to see her off.

Bagila's father not only did not respond to the stranger's mean greeting, but he was also genuinely surprised at his presence in the compartment and stared into the guy's face for several seconds, then pointedly asked in bewilderment: "Is your seat here?!" - in such a tone, as if the stranger was not worthy even to stand next to him. The young man, with his former cold calmness, laid out newspapers and magazines on a small table, pushing Bagila at the same time, and answered with a caustic smile: "Yes, my seat is here, right where you're sitting." His direct cold gaze was so sharp that it seemed to pierce through the interlocutor.

For a brief moment, Karatai was crushed by some frightening inner strength of the stranger, but then, after quickly pulling himself together, he assumed the posture of a dominant person with indifferent calmness and went out into the corridor.

"If I'm not mistaken, that's your father," the guy suddenly spoke, and without looking at Bagila, he continued to leaf through the newspapers. "I just want to understand, is he taking you to school? He seems like one of those people who strive to ensure that their daughter enters a university at any cost, I can tell just by looking at him. Undoubtedly, it seems that he did not like me very much." The man's tone touched Bagila, she almost exploded with indignation and began to bite her lips.

But the guy was imperturbable and still sat, buried in his newspapers. Bagila was not accustomed to such neglect and was even taken aback by her own resentment and indignation, not knowing how to behave further with this terrible person. More than anything in the world, she wanted her father to return as soon as possible and save her from this painful state, so that he would take her away from this rude man, whose look and words were angrier than dry thorns. As if guessing the thoughts of his daughter and hurrying to protect her from trouble, her father entered the compartment. He was not alone. Behind him was one of the leaders of the district who had come to see him off, the head of the station, the foreman of the train, and some other people. Seeing a calm, self-confident father, hearing his low, sedate voice, Bagila was so delighted, as if she had escaped from the encirclement of enemies and found herself in an impregnable fortress. Never before had she loved her father so much, and never has she been so grateful to him and proud of him, as she was now.

The people who arrived with her father made a thousand apologies; they asked the young man to move to another compartment. The man's swarthy face turned white with anger. Karatai seemed pleased. The guy pointedly looked at Karatai's retinue, who were pushing him from all sides. Karatai saw that he had driven his zealous fellow traveller into a corner, he saw that fury and despair were seething in his eyes. Bagila gloatingly watched the stranger suffer. "That's what you get, now you know what happens if you mess with us again!"

The guy lowered his eyes, and the retinue fell silent, believing that he would take the suitcase and leave. But he did not think to rush. At this time, the red-haired head of the station, pretty frightened by all this commotion, Karatai's bad mood and the fact that the truth was on the side of the rebellious young man, seized a second and whispered something in the man's ear.

The stranger didn't even raise an eyebrow. Seeing that words had no effect on him, the head of the station was truly frightened. Curving in some strange, unpleasant bow, he whispered to him once more. Bagila caught a humiliating plea in the whisper.

The stranger slowly stood up. Slowly began to collect his newspapers and things. Then he looked around at everyone in turn, as if he were standing in front of columns, not people.

"Whatever... I feel sorry for your subordinates...

And you too," he said quietly but distinctly to Karatai and moved through the retinue, behind the head of the station.

Karatai sank heavily onto his seat. There was no triumph on his face, not even satisfaction. On the contrary, Bagila understood this, he painfully worried about the words of the random man.

When the man was leaving the compartment, Bagila finally got a good look at him. As long as he took the suitcase with him, the girl wanted him to disappear quickly, and then, as if a beam of light fell on an ice floe frozen in her soul, she looked at him with pity. And again, she looked into his eyes, in the expression of his face, in his entire posture, the painful pride, the eternal fear of being hurt and offended, and Bagila experienced surprise and compassion for the stranger at the same time.

The train started moving. Only now Bagila noticed that there were a lot of people who were seeing off her father. She knew everyone too, but it was somehow embarrassing to see them together on the station platform, at the same time, as if on command, they were waving to one person - her father.

"Dad, are you tired?" Bagila asked, unable to endure the heavy silence that arose in the compartment after the man left.

The father looked at his daughter with a smile, as if he wanted to say: "Don't worry about that nonsense!" -

and shook his head negatively, but his eyes were sad.

An attendant came and changed Karatai's bed again. When the attendant took hold of the pillowcase, a sheet of paper was found underneath. One side of it was completely written on. The guide tossed the sheet onto the table, as if making it clear that at the moment there was nothing more important than changing the pillowcase. Karatai didn't see any importance in the fact that someone's notes were found in his compartment.

Bagila did not yet know and could not know that there was only one step from love to hate and vice versa, but from that moment she felt that all her attention had shifted to the sheet of written paper. What could this sharp, handsome young man write about, the man who so easily offended her and her father? What thoughts did he entrust to this sheet? She was convinced that in the lines that covered the white sheet there were words, expressions, thoughts completely different from those that she heard, read, knew until today. It couldn't be anything else!

Suddenly a new thought appeared, flashing like lightning, electrifying her mind. Bagila shuddered and began to breathe rapidly. "He might come back to us for the forgotten paper!"

Bagila did not know whether she wanted or did not want the stranger to appear again, she was afraid to understand this, but one thing was clear: her quiet life, which had been flowing for all eighteen years in the family cradle of respect and reverence, dignity and fame, was shaken up today, like a bird after sleep.

"Dad, are you thirsty? I'll bring you tea!" Bagila said loudly, as if trying to scare away her current state, into the clutches of which she fell without resisting, and now she decided that she would easily be able to get rid of this new feeling, she had only to speak up, to say something... Her father answered in a sleepy voice that he did not want tea but instead he wants to lie down a bit and think about business.

The compartment door quietly slid aside, and a male voice came from the corridor: "May I?"

Bagila almost flew off her seat. A man – a completely different man - raised his eyebrows, surprised at such a panicky fright of the girl. And her cheeks instantly flushed.

"Karatai Isaevich, do you need anything at the moment?" the man asked, as if explaining the purpose of his arrival.

Karatai repeated what he had said to his daughter without turning his face away from the wall. The young man hastily apologised and disappeared, silently closing the door behind him. It was only later, Bagila learnt that two guys were traveling with them in the next compartment, but were they travelling on the road for their own business or were they there to accompany her father? This she did not know.

"Dad, you rest, and I will stand in the corridor..."

"As you wish." A slight irritation slipped through his father's voice; he didn't like it when people interfered with his rest. "Although you should rest too..."

Bagila went out into the corridor and saw her native steppe through the open window. It swam back majestically, splashing towards the horizon in gentle, lazily rounded hills. Looking at it, one might think that the whole world is a great undulating space without a single sharp line. At first glance, any person, even if you were to tie them with a hair lasso, could not linger in this hot sleepy steppe for very long and would run away to wherever their eyes looked, breaking any restrains they might have. And sometimes she herself was not far from thinking of doing the same. But last year, having rested for a month in Crimea, then touring the Baltic republics and returning home a week before the start of the school year, she suddenly felt with all her heart, how much she dearly loved this outwardly plain steppe land of hers. For a long time, she remembered the Black Sea and the Baltic, but each time the boundless strong water passed in her mind into her native hilly steppe, the charms of the sea and forest were clouded by the calm, soft beauty of the immense feather grass plain on which she was born and grew up.

"Do you like the steppe?" A sweet, ingratiating voice rang out from behind her.

Turning around, Bagila saw a jigit horseman with an ingratiating smile on his face, the same one who had offered services to his father a minute ago. His name was Turgat. And again, an obliging readiness showed through in his behaviour, as if at any moment he would say, "What are my orders? I will execute them immediately." It seems that this is a well-groomed man, always carefully watching himself, striving to appear affable, understanding, and intelligent in front of people. Bagila often saw him next to her father, but not once did she manage to understand what thoughts, what essence is hidden behind the man's fake smile, his helpfulness, his feigned culture. In order to somehow understand Turgat, one has to look deep into his eyes, carefully, but Bagila could not decide on such a thing. On the contrary, when meeting with him, she either turned aside, as if not noticing him, or greeted him without raising her head. And he always smiled no matter what happened around him. And now he was blooming in an especially welcoming smile, as if he had heard something pleasant from Bagila. She had never had a heart for him, but Bagila understood that for the sake of decency it was necessary to say something in response.

"Look…" she said in a barely audible voice.

"Oh, the steppe is always wonderful and unique! But nothing can compare with Almaty! If you don't mind, I'll show you the city when we arrive. I know Almaty by heart!"

"I also know Almaty… well enough," said Bagila somewhat harshly, deciding to stop the flow of his words, which began to rush down like a stream from a steep.

"Ah, is that how it is? That's a bold statement, it is difficult to really 'know' Almaty, especially its surroundings. You know, Almaty is precisely beautiful in the outskirts," said Turgat.

"Probably."

"I studied there for five years. Yes, I was born and grew up near the city. If I say something wrong, I beg your pardon, but it's probably because I'm going to my fatherland... I hope it doesn't all pass through you, a draft like that would be a terrible thing for a person..."

Bagila sighed as if she had to swallow something sugary and sticky.

"Thanks, I'll make sure it won't."

"You still take care." He looked at the girl as if he were her own older brother. "Of course, everyone cherishes their fatherland. You are young at the moment, but you will understand what I am talking about later. To be honest, at first, I wanted to escape from this place back to my homeland. But one thing kept me, my shame before Karatai Isaevich. And now I'm used to it, I've made up my mind about everything... But I still yearn for my homeland. You haven't experienced anything like this…"

Bagila could not overcome her disgust for Turgat. She didn't want to talk at all.

She quietly went to the compartment where her father was resting. Turgat stood like a monument, offended by the neglect of the girl. Bagila felt awkward and, after taking a few steps, turned to him.

"Excuse me... a stranger who was in our compartment left some paper. If it's not difficult, can you tell him about it?" She said pleadingly.

Turgat forgot his grudge against Bagila in the blink of an eye and looked at her with a smile.

"I will gladly do it with all my heart... You know that I am always ready to serve you."

Instead of a grimace of ambition and resentment, a smile settled on his face, ready to be in the wings of a person. But Bagila knew that the fury of pride had not yet cooled down in him, and she was struck by his rare ability to control himself in accordance with the situation and to suppress all emotions in himself, if necessary. True, the reason for this change in his mood was most likely something else, that this guy was from the breed of those who simply cannot be offended, but Bagila somehow did not think about it. If she had looked at him, she would have seen a respectful smile, such respect that she would have wanted to pat the guy on the shoulder, but Bagila looked at his black patent leather shoes instead.

"No, I don't need you to serve me, it would be better if you provided service to that person," she said dryly and went into the compartment.

Her father was sleeping. From an old habit, he snored softly and monotonously, with his mouth slightly open. Bagila remembered how her grandmother, who had died a few years ago, would actively go around the rooms and wake up everyone who was snoring. She approached them, stepping inaudibly, gently touching their shoulder, while saying "Turn to the other side." While she was waking to another one, the one whom grandmother had just laid on their side was snoring again, and she again hurried back to them. So, until sleep overcame her, the grandmother paced back and forth between her children and grandchildren. "Grandma, why are you waking up those who are snoring?" Bagila asked. "A demon strangles a person at night. That's why they snore," she answered. Whether because the terrible words of her grandmother had been firmly planted in her mind since childhood, or because she was accustomed to rest in silence, always in a separate room, but Bagila could not stand it when someone snored nearby. Like her grandmother, she quietly approached and was about to wake her father, but then she again saw a half-written sheet of paper on the table and froze in place, again experiencing a new, strange feeling...

She slowly reached out and picked up the sheet. Her breath hitched, it seemed that her father woke up. She looked at him. He was asleep, though he was no longer snoring. She looked back at the paper in relief, the words written seemed completely different from what she imagined. The writer seemed to be bullying someone, not really thinking about how smart his position was. She re-read it several times before the writing began to reach her...

"Admiration and worship have never belonged to abstract concepts, since the very final analysis they are connected with the worldview of an individual. And the personality itself, its consciousness and thought are always concrete... The prose of Thackeray, Hugo, Frans, Schiller Scott that are known to the whole world did not arouse admiration and worship in me. Probably, someone is ready to attack me for this knowledge, and they say, that this is almost sedition! Yes, where did this wisdom come from, on what basis did he... and so on. So, they are fans. The ones who admire him can be dissuaded, the flame of their adoration can be knocked down, but the admirers cannot be turned off their path. It looks like a cult, fanaticism. Fanaticism and reason cannot live side by side, they are incompatible concepts. If fanaticism flourishes in an environment of ignorance, then reason develops in a conscious society. I do not bow before the writers mentioned above, I do not even admire them, because many can write like that. On the contrary, most of all I am attracted by the philosophical concepts of the little-known P. Borel, who lived in the eighteenth century, who died at the age of twenty-three. Surprising and striking is his unexpected approach to many issues, a kind of desire to make a revolution in the minds of people. Or the modern Russian writer D. Granin! His "This Strange Life" (the rest is weak) stands high! The sensational Rasputin and Astafiev are worth attention, but they did not add anything new to the universal thought. 'Somebody' named R. Vaillant excites me in a completely new way. Because he knows how to criticise himself boldly and sharply. And if we evaluate Kazakh literature, the professional level of its artistic prose and artistic thinking..."

...Bagila sat without taking her eyes off the paper. She did not know how to react to what she read, to admire or toss the sheet away like garbage. But is it really possible to admire something from now on if he writes that admiration and worship ultimately lead to ease in assessments. True, this is not a very clear concept, but what if what he wrote is the truth itself?! And if it's not?

She remembered Turgat, who remained standing in the corridor. She smiled contemptuously, thinking again about his ignorance and narcissism, about how he puts forward his chest, in which a false conscience nests.

And the one who wrote these lines? Undoubtedly, he is completely different! Up until that moment she had felt a sense of mocking pity for the man her father had sent out of the compartment, but now this arrogant feeling has been replaced by bitter shame. She did not know who he was, but she understood: he was much higher than them, including her father, higher than all those people among whom she had lived until now. It became unpleasant for her that she somehow imperceptibly placed a man she met by chance above her father; even angry at herself for this, Bagila admitted that it was so. Even if what he wrote was a complete delusion, though those words themselves, the particular train of thought, were completely unattainable for the father. But, Lord, it turned out to be disgusting to admit someone else's superiority, how unbearable it was to admit that the will of her father, manifested in relation to a stranger, was nothing more than the tyranny of a power-hungry man. "So does my father really think that the strength of power can take precedence over knowledge, over the mind?!" Bagila marvelled at this idea.

"He who thinks, has no joy in life." This poetic line, which for some unknown reason had sunk into her memory, now continually sounded in her head, disturbing her. "How strange," she thought, "Why did Abai say that there is no joy for a thinker?! After all, a thinking and just person always wins in the end, the truth will be on his side, he will taste the fruits of his labour, his knowledge, his thoughts. And we are told this at every corner, as far as I can remember myself, we have been taught this for ten years. So, who do I trust: Abai or my teachers? And how can you not trust the other?!"

"He who thinks, has no joy in life..."

Bagila's mind was all jumbled up. Her consciousness became unsteady, like a mirage in the steppe, and she did not know what thought to grasp. And they were frighteningly sharp for her, pushing for grades that she could not even dare before. Something strange was happening to her. After all, a few hours ago everything was so calm, unshakable and, as it seemed to her, good.

Now, no matter what she thought about, her thoughts ran into some kind of dead end, and this dead end for her became a stranger who casually scolded Hugo, who was thrown out of the compartment by her father, like an unnecessary newspaper. Of course, losing your seat in a compartment is not a great loss, not the worst mockery. But why, why did her father need to be violent? She looked at her father, who was sleeping, her mouth parted so that blackness gaped behind her teeth, and once again, she cautiously touched the sheet that lay in front of her on the table with her fingers. And what's next?

A painful desire arose in her - it was imperative, that at any cost, she had to find out what was written in the other sheets. Was that all she wanted? Well, of course, she also wanted to read the beginning or end of these arguments and see this man again, talk to him.

This time, the opportunity to appear in front of the man did not frighten her...

The train arrived in Almaty in the evening. And here her father had many acquaintances. Despite the unbearable July heat, five men in full dress suits and ties enthusiastically greeted them at the station and led them to two brand new Volgas.

Their car sped along a beautiful street lined with silvery poplars. The sun was long gone, and the sky is still pink, broken in the south by snow-white mountain peaks. The avenue was watered a few minutes ago, and the wheels of the Volga were throwing back the mirrored asphalt with a wet whistle.

The voices behind her did not stop for a second. Bagila heard that their conversation was chaotic, it was about everything at once. One of the greeters began to tell that in the summer it is more profitable to fly by plane. He was actually in Tashkent recently, he got on a plane, and then – he arrived without any road torment. Then, with some greed, he talked about the shish kebabs, which are allegedly sold in Tashkent at every turn. "One has only to go out into the street, as the tablecloth is already out laid in front of you," he exclaimed dreamily. "As long as you have some roubles, you can eat your fill!" The storyteller seemed to have arrived from a distant unknown country and therefore did not know that those sitting in the car had been to Tashkent at least five or six times already...

Bagila stared intently at the white stripes on the pavement flying under the car, and wondered to herself: how can such mature, respectable people talk with pleasure about some petty, meaningless things, laugh, downright laugh where there is nothing to laugh at, even at the slightest things.

The cars in front stopped next to a six-story building in the very centre of the city, they were so close they were basically squeezing each other. The owner of the apartment building turned out to be a lean, tall, middle-aged man with thick grey hair beyond his age, the same one who had been talking about his trip to Tashkent all the way over here without a break. When they noisily entered the apartment, they were met by a beautiful swarthy hostess of about thirty, smiling shyly at the door.

"Oh, Malika, how are you?" Exclaimed her father, and Bagila realised that this woman was the wife of the fan of Tashkent shish kebabs.

Quickly wiping her hands on her apron, she embraced her father, saying:

"Oh, Karatai, it turns out you're here as well!" She rushed to serve the guests slippers. "You used to come often, but then you became the boss - and disappeared before our eyes. Have you gained any weight? Well let me see!" She began to examine Karatai from all sides. "No, looks like your stomach still isn't ahead of you." But remember, the first head of the district should not be thinner than necessary."

"Malika, don't forget that we have another distinguished guest in our house today," the owner said sternly to his wife, who, in his opinion, was too carried away by Karatai. She turned to Bagila, who was quiet in the corner of the corridor.

"Oh goodness, how lovely! Beautiful! I remember your name is Bagila?" Maliki gave her a quick kiss on the cheek. "Indeed, it is not time that ages a person, but those who they grow up next to, next to this beauty I am quite an old woman, eh! When I saw her about two years ago, she was a girl busy with dolls, but now look, she's so charming!" Malika chirped.

"Malika, I think we will have enough time to philosophise on the topic of the transience of life," the husband said, and Bagila caught that the topic of old age greatly offended him. It turns out interestingly, that even though they haven't had time to sit down yet, the husband has already pulled his wife back twice.

"And what is left for us but to philosophise?" Malika continued playfully, not thinking of changing her tone. "A person who has seen a lot, who has experienced a lot, philosophises, but I'm not a girl," she exclaimed cheerfully, and everyone understood that it was too early for her to show off. "All right, come to the table."

At the table the conversation was as twitchy as in the car. They talked at the same time about the weather, politics, about the appointment of one person and the dismissal of another, then, as expected, they returned to the Tashkent shish kebab. Bagila did not understand this table conversation very well. There was nothing unexpected in their words, nothing new that could remain in her memory, or that would touch the soul. She often visited such dinner tables with her parents, where people of various kinds met. At first, she was surprised by the similarity of words, jokes and laughter of the people sitting at these tables, she was especially surprised because people did not resemble each other, at least in name and surname, in appearance and behaviour, in position...

But over time she was so accustomed to this that she no longer automatically delved into their conversations. She found a good way to spend time at such tables: look at people, smile and think about her own things. And this time, as she sipped her thick brown tea mixed with milk, she kept her eyes on the bookshelves that lined both of the long walls of the living room, making the room look more like a small library. And at the table they laughed loudly, smacked their lips, chewed, and somehow this image did not fit in with the bookshelves behind them, it even seemed to Bagila as some kind of sacrilege. She looked for a moment at the owner of the house, who, picking his teeth, spoke with pleasure about the cock-fights held in Tashkent. She kept her eyes on him: a fair-faced man with prominent cheekbones, shifty eyes with a kind of crazy gleam, a sharp nose, thin lips. Bagila felt uncomfortable. She had already met such people and at the same time noticed that they were petty scrupulous, irritable, always predisposed to an argument, jealous and arrogant at the same time. On top of that, they are too cautious and ready to fawn. Without taking her eyes off that mobile, nervously cheerful face, she suddenly wondered: had the owner of the house read all these books?

"Bagila, your tea is cold, give me your cup," came a voice from her right side, and, looking there, she saw Turgat.

'God, he's annoying! It's so stuffy, and yet he sits in a jacket like a doll! Can't he wipe the sweat off his forehead!' Bagila felt her alienation towards this man grow into almost disgusted contempt. She furrowed her eyebrows and did not think of holding out her cup to him. Turgat decided that Bagel was embarrassed by the unfamiliar situation, and he himself took her cup, giving it to Malika, who was pouring tea.

"Malika, don't make it too hot. Add more milk. Bagila loves it like that…" he said in a business-like way, in a sweetly soft, caressing voice.

'That's how it is!' Bagila was angry. 'Why is he pretending to be a supporter?'

"No, let it be hot," she asked. Turgat did not lose his head and immediately showed that he perfectly knows all the desires and weaknesses of Bagila.

"Yes, yes, it can be a bit hot. When she gets tired from a long journey, she likes hot tea," he explained with perfect calmness.

'Insolent!' Bagila was furious. 'He thinks something will burn him out!'

There was a red-hot seven-litre electric samovar, the breaths of people steamed with meat and vodka, the sparkle of two huge crystal chandeliers, six lamps each, which could decorate the hall of a small theatre, the room had turned into a real bathhouse.

There was a huge fan, placed on the windowsill, which hummed straining, wanting to serve the feast, but it only mixed the damp stuffiness of the room with its rubber blades, which smelled of smoked meat and alcohol. Karatai, quietly rising from his seat, took off his grey summer jacket, threw it on the back of a chair, and threw his tie on a small coffee table. Then he unbuttoned the top two buttons of his shirt, took a deep breath, as if he had lifted a heavy weight from his shoulders, and sank into a chair in relief.

Bagila looked away from the books, she looked at the people at the table and saw that everyone was sitting in shirts. Turgat also took off his jacket and sat, imitating her father, whilst unbuttoning the top two buttons on his shirt. Bagila could not understand how adults who had known each other for a long time, having met at the table, so easily became prisoners of some stupid conventions.

Each of those present has already made their toast.

All words their wishes were similar to each other, as well as thoughts that were generously shared with each other at this table. Even Turgat, who did his best to appear well-educated and cultured, mumbled some boring tirade about friendship. Those who sat at the table were taught restraint, they listened to everything, and as soon as Turgat finished, everyone moved and began to thank him so fervently, as if from the day of their birth they had not heard deeper wisdom. Then Karatai raised his glass to Malika's health, to her unfading beauty. These words excited the guests again.

Only the owner of the house, Sargel, brought his thin lips closer to the crystal rim of his glass, as if wondering if they were going to poison him in his own house, and tasted the cognac with the tip of his tongue, smacking his lips. At the same time, his face remained motionless, Surged was clearly not at ease. So, he protested to his wife because she drank cognac to the bottom in front of people. Malika didn't care about the protest. Her husband simply did not exist for her now. Sargel closed his hand over his glass and squeezed it with his fist so violently that Bagila was afraid that the glass would splatter in all directions.

Bile was clearly accumulating on both sides. At the same time, Malika did not at all give in to her jealous and suspicious husband. It seems that everyone at the table managed to figure out that the hostile relationship between the host and hostess arose through the fault of Sargel. If his wife did not pay attention to anyone, especially men, if she did not look at the sweets that were offered to her and defiantly sit down before him with the air of a woman who has cooled down, if she had not been fond of anyone for a long time, if she does not need anyone apart from her husband, Sargel's mood would be great. But unfortunately, such moments were rare, especially in recent times. No matter how jealous her husband was, no matter how furious he got, Malika did not even think to restrain herself. She had long understood that her husband was incapable of action, that there was not even a shadow of determination in him, the ability to make any decisions, to act sharply, authoritatively, like other men. Sargel was well aware of his flaws. The consciousness of his own weakness corroded her from the inside, and sharpened his nerves and brain. At such moments, he literally fell ill, became frighteningly nervous, suspicious.

Malika was the exact opposite of him. On long evenings, the husband would be shuffling soft room slippers, paced between the study, the dining room and the kitchen, muttering about something with displeasure, whilst Malika behaved in accordance with her mood, not even trying to change her husband's state of mind for the better. At first, Sargel did not miss the opportunity to demonstrate offended pride, however, he did this as a rule, in silence. He understood that he could yell at his wife, even give her a thrashing, he knew that such behaviour - yelling, even beating - would not do him any good, on the contrary, mutual hatred would spill out, their confrontation would become open, and so to avoid a breakup – he keeps his hands back. And at this age, in which Sargel is, an open struggle could only promise him defeat. And he was forced to choose another kind of resistance – silent discontent. Over the years, this position of his became completely helpless, and gradually he began to obey the wishes of his wife. To obey involuntarily, with the hopelessness of a desperate person. But Malika did not consider this a victory, she was so confident in herself, as if she knew for sure that her will would triumph in this house, she was perplexed why her husband did not give up so quickly. Malika could not be dissuaded from the fact that only her priority is the condition for complete mutual understanding in the family.

In their married life, from the very first minute, the sovereignty of one person protruded - Malika. She responded to her husband's anger with poisonous correctness. With all of her behaviour - in the kitchen at tea, next to the TV, in bed - she slowly, deliberately peacefully, like a child, explained to him the inappropriateness of his jealousy, said that with his malicious jealousy he insulted her dignity. But as such Sargel, by nature, could not live without suspicion. And yet, no matter how jealousy tormented Sargel, no matter how he tortured himself with suspicion, like the unsteady shadow of a willow tree or the light of a lonely lamp in a distant village, he was sometimes calmed by a flickering ray of faith. For the last three or four months, this ray has become, as it were, stronger. Sargel came home from work unusually early several times and found his wife either washing clothes, or she was making jam, preparing compote for the winter, happily devoting herself to these female family duties. After such idyllic pictures, his heart became calm. Twice, unexpectedly for himself, Sargel arrived from a business trip ahead of schedule (the last time from Tashkent). Yes, even late at night. Malika slept with her children on either side. He opened the door himself, with his own key. Before waking up his wife, he examined the apartment for any suspicious traces. Everything seemed to be in order. Even the ashtray, which he had glanced at unnoticed by his wife after his arrival, was in the same place, by the hanger, and in it, as before, lay the only burnt match. Around were scattered children's things, toys, drawings. There was a peaceful silence in the house. Even when he, having entered the bedroom, turned on the light and the chandelier flared up, Malika did not wake up from the sharp click or from an unexpected flash of light. And this, according to Sargel, spoke of the complete peace of mind of his wife. Inappropriate suspicions were dispelled in him, and he even became ashamed of his jealousy.

His life began to enter a well-fed, quiet course, he was already satisfied with everything in the world, and then suddenly today's feast came around...

Looking at the rapidly moving, cheerful wife (she was clinking glasses with the guests at that moment), Sargel felt with hopeless longing: his thoughts were again filled with the poison of distrust, giving rise to an unbearably painful state. It was at that moment that he clearly understood that he would never believe his wife, his soul would never be calm, and his love would be completely crushed by blind jealousy.

Six years ago, he lost his wife, his first... No one else felt guilty of her death more than Sargel. Her heart was too weak for Sargel. If the wife went to the store on the way home for groceries and did not return at the time appointed by her husband, and if during the day the home phone was busy when he called from the office, Sargel would chew-out his wife and torture her with sarcastic questions: "Who kept you?", "Who did you meet in the store?", "Which donkey confessed their feelings to you on the phone?" This would happen several times, unable to bear the remarks, her heart seized, and she lost consciousness. Over time, his wife stopped going out to meetings with him, so that a quarrel would not break out in the house the next day. He didn't get tired of making scandals. Even when they were sitting in front of the TV, he would suddenly start yelling: "Why are you staring at the announcer?"

Their life ended with the fact that during another scandal, she fainted in the kitchen and the ambulance took his wife to the hospital. When the next day he came to visit her with the two children, it turned out that his wife was no longer alive. Her note was handed to him: "Take the children to my relatives. I'm leaving. If you're so jealous, come to me…"

Pain rang in his temples. Through this pain, he did not hear the children crying out loud and calling for their mother.

The last words of his wife were long stored in his memory. One day he realised with horror that only by her death she was able to prove his guilt to him, that until now, without attaching importance to what jealousy could lead to, he slowly tortured her and eventually killed her. He killed her…

At first, he was tormented, even a certainty arose that he would never recover from this unexpected blow, but five or six months passed, and the grief suddenly faded away easily, a blush played on Sargel's face again. When meeting with friends, he joked. The tense mood gave way to fun without resisting. Previously, when his wife was alive, he walked as if lowered into water, there was nothing in his head but suspicions and jealousy, but now, freed from her, he was freed from jealousy, it became easy, free. True, sometimes some distant and almost cold feeling of guilt pricked him, at that moment it hurt, and it was hard under his heart, but time went on and on, and finally that feeling of the cold edge died down, and nothing bothered him, nothing interferes with life, it was as he wanted.

A year later, he married Malika. She had been married once before him. Her husband played the drum in the orchestra of one of the prestigious restaurants in Almaty. When he met her, he introduced himself as a composer. Looking at his long, poorly combed hair, huge beard, listening to stories about music, Malika considered it quite possible. At that time, she worked as a saleswoman in the Bereke national food store. The 'composer' did not drag out the whole 'acquaintance' thing, a month later he proposed to get married. To reject the young talent, who was still unfortunately, quite unlucky in life, was beyond Malika's strength, and she agreed. Before marriage, it was necessary to introduce the future husband to her parents.

She took him to their house, which stood in the suburbs of Almaty. When the hairy groom stepped on the threshold of the parental home, the children, busy playing, fled to the corners. The old women, who, in anticipation of the bridegroom, were sitting, talking less and less, they could not turn their tongues from surprise.

The youth gathered, when the evening reached a certain intensity, the groom showed his art. Coming out to the middle, he began to dance like crazy and suddenly yelled:

"Drum! Give me a drum!"

"Why does he need a drum, huh?" Malika's father asked and licked his instantly dry lips.

"Give me a drum! I wrote a drum concerto!"

Malika's father was in charge of the educational department at the school. He sent some boys for the drum.

The 'Concerto for a drum without an orchestra' lasted until three in the morning.

The wedding ceremony took place in a restaurant. Only at the wedding did Malika find out that her husband was not a composer at all, but a simple drummer at the Tastak restaurant. This was told to her by one of the guests invited by the groom.

Married life from the very first night began coldly. Three months later, they were both quite content with their divorce. An unsuccessful marriage broke Malika. After that, men appeared before her, but they were all ready for anything, but not for marriage, and she began to stay away from them. Time passed. She was twenty-eight. She felt how every day the ideal that she had dreamed of and hoped to meet was moving further and further away from her, how the flame of youth was weakening along with the passing years.

Peers of the same age got married a long time ago, and some unmarried women are cunning people who know how to fool their heads with pleasure for themselves. The men she met would call her on the second day after they met, and with no shame at all, ask her to get 'kazy', 'zhaya' and other national delicacies from horse meat. It hurt her painfully and gave rise to squeamish hostility. She despised the pettiness of men. "But where are all the horsemen?!" She often asked herself. "Where did the real men go?" If they are all like that, then why get married at all?! Or do the real ones manage to get wives before the age of thirty?

All of her acquaintances with men convinced Malika that the everyman she's ever met only cared for wine, food, fun and their bed. These four concepts were the boundaries of their lives. Every single one. It is completely incomprehensible why they go out of their way to get into at least some institute and get a diploma? Do you need a higher education to drink wine and lie in bed with women?

She met Sargel at the exact moment when she was more than ever angry with all men, She noticed him before, he often perused the store. Malika even noticed that lately he had been somewhat incomprehensibly rejuvenated, he became collected, energetic. She did not know where and by whom he worked. He wasn't too old, although his hair is touched with a bit of grey, he was most likely wealthy. Somehow the store received camel milk. The store sold it for three days, and on the fourth day the milk disappeared so instantly, as if Allah had cleaned up all the camels at once.

But it was the three-day camel milk trade that introduced them. At first, Sargel ran into the store every day - he loved camel milk. Then they agreed to meet after work. Leaving the store, Malika saw Sargel standing by the payphone booth, waiting, frozen as if he had been put on a wooden corset. Malika, laughing, approached him, loudly tapping her heels.

"Oh, it's you? Hello! Waiting for me?"

"Oh no! For a girl like you, I'll be happy to wait without closing my eyes until dawn!" said Sargel somewhat pompously.

"Then you'll be happy for six whole days!"

"Hmm, I don't understand," he said with a forced smile.

"We have five girls here who are like me, so six of us in total."

"Oh my!" Sargel was falsely delighted, throwing back his head and loudly, as if in a drum, clapping his hands.

From such an unexpected and unpleasant movement, Malika broke off her laughter and looked at him in surprise.

"What a miracle! Well, you're quite the joker! You scared me. Are you a composer by any chance?"

"No. I'm an assistant professor! A historian."

"Oh, a scientist then!"

Malika hooked up with Sargel out of idle interest for the sake of spending time, but quietly got used to his attitude. Moreover, the historian took on all the costs of the wedding and she began to perceive him without alienation, his grey hair, his manner of speaking, his emphasis on every word, him holding his body as if it were carved out of wood, him to moving his head when walking, him looking at people meaningfully, searchingly.

She got used to his jacket and tie, which he wore despite the unbearable heat, to the French perfume that spread a sickening smell, to his scrupulous and zealous character, and even to undisguised stinginess. She got used to all this without difficulty because all these qualities met in different combinations in young and old men with whom she was familiar, and Sargel's character was not a surprise to Malika. In addition, Sargel simply captivated her by the fact that the next day after they met, he did not call with a request to get some kind of deficit, did not begin to dissolve his hands against the expectation. Malika was not afraid at his house, she liked it. The apartment was located in the very centre of the city and consisted of five spacious rooms. The rooms were full of imported furniture, the bookshelves were full of books, the parquet floor gleamed like a mirror. The cleanliness, pedantic accuracy of the owner, the fact that he is a respected assistant professor - everything, everything led her to the following thought: "In what way is he worse than the young ones? And which way are they better than him? On the contrary, he does not drink, does not lie, he has everything in sight. In addition, he does not go with me just for the sake of having fun in bed."

As soon as this thought appeared in her head, it began to occupy Malika's mind every day, more and more often, and not only during meetings with Sargel... Every day she was more and more persistently fascinated by pictures of a calm family life, the joy of having children, her own hearth. The only thing was that she could not determine her attitude towards Sargel's two children, who remained from his first wife, she had a vague premonition that they would dispel the calmness of future relationships, would cool the warmth of the house that she would raise with Sargel. Sargel understood these thoughts of hers without unnecessary hints and took the children to his wife's close relatives. He took them, promising that he would come and visit, he sends money on time and brings them to the city for the holidays...

And so, they got married. Karatai was also invited to the wedding ceremony. At that time, Karatai worked only as a director of a state farm. Their fathers' fathers were closely related. He came to the wedding ceremony with good gifts. Moreover, he took care of all the expenses for the wedding. It was not in vain that Sargel noticed Karatai from all the distant and close relatives...

This year, when Karatai's daughter, after graduating from high school, wished to continue her studies, Sargel wrote a letter to Karatai saying that the time had come for him to repay good for good, he himself would arrange for Bagila to go to university and that, if necessary, she could live in his apartment.

They drunk cognac, the stuffiness somewhat crushed the guests, Karat noticed how Sargel had more wrinkles on his forehead, how often his thin lips began to tighten, how he spoke less and less, because Malika was getting more and more cheerful. He did not follow how much his young wife drank; he was not interested. Whilst hiding the fact, he admired her open character, her beautiful face, on which a passionate blush always smouldered, eyes black as a currant berry sparkled, piercing through a person with a magical mysterious light. But, noticing Sargel's inner tension, Karatai tried to answer Malika's playful questions indifferently, calmly and coolly. This attitude towards the wife soon bore fruit. Sargel, like a sleepy child, carefully looked around, came to life and began to join in on the jokes and table conversations. Karatai was delighted that at such an important moment for Bagila, his relative and friend liked him, he was able to stop Malika's fun and direct the feast in the right direction for Sargel.

Malika, noticing how tired Bagila looked, took her away from the table to a separate room. The two sons of Sargel used to live in this room. Now it was empty. The windows were curtained with light yellow silk curtains, and in the right corner, near a folding soft sofa, stood a yellowish floor lamp, matching the colour of the curtains. Imported bookshelves lined the opposite wall in two rows, with a stuffed deer head gathering dust above them. His glassy eyes, that gleaming from the yellowish light of the floor lamp, looked sad and reproachfully assessed everything that was happening in the small desolate world of this apartment. The head didn't know and didn't seem to want to know who shot it and why they did, or where it's body had gone, why it hung here, on the wall of the capital's apartment. Now the most important thing for these yellow eyes was to look at the owners of the apartment, to see how they live, how they tortured each other.

"If you want, you can open the window," said Malika. "It's quiet on this side, there are no cars. Well, get settled. This room will be yours. Here are some modern records. You can play any of them if you want. Don't be shy, make yourself at home. I love open people. We will still chat with you from the heart. In the meantime, I'll go tend to the guests. Deal?"

Bagila smiled and nodded to her hostess.

The room was cool and dim. The noise of the feast,

the clinking of dishes in the hall barely reached. She immediately noticed that after her departure everyone felt freer, and stung by this, she thought that there was absolutely no reason to sit for so long, drowning in tobacco smoke among unnecessary conversations.

Bagila, sighing deeply in relief, sat down on the sofa, leaning back. Her gaze rested on the books that filled the shelves. All the books were brand new and clearly unread. She looked towards the door and walked over to the shelves. She took one of the books, read the title: "Aesthetics of Hellenism." Opened it up. The pages crunched loudly, as if expressing dissatisfaction for the disturbance, and as she slowly opened, some pages would be stuck together in dozens. She listed through a few pages with her long fingernail and began to read at random. The letters were small, the words were written with tension. She skimmed through half a page quickly. Understood nothing. It simply did not reach her consciousness. She put the book back. Sat on the sofa. She mechanically raised her head and saw the dried head of a deer above her. His eyes were so large, as if open with terror. Bagila trembled all over, her heart went cold. She jumped up and quickly lit a large chandelier. The head was still looking at her, but now the eyes were shallow and cloudy. She, having calmed down, sat down in her place, but did not extinguish the chandelier. From road fatigue, table noise and her temple painfully pounding with blood, Bagila comfortably arranged a pillow that lay in the middle of the sofa, slowly and quietly, as if afraid to wake someone up, she lay down on it, carefully straightened her skirt with her hands, which slightly bared her knees, and covered her eyes. The sharp light of the chandelier, that was pointing straight down, straight into her face, quickly faded, subsiding and gradually went out completely.

She slept for over an hour. The bright light falling from above, reflected from the light, yellow curtains of the window, and gently set off Bagila's elusive swarthy face. Her swiftly arched eyebrows, very similar to the silhouette of a black seagull flying forwards, harmoniously combined with a semicircle of closed eyelashes, which gave rise to an exciting line, as if asserting that nature itself is an unsurpassed artist. The chest, indicated under the white blouse, was lifting easily and imperceptibly to the eye. Now at this moment, Bagila's appearance was the answer to the eternal question of mankind: what is beauty and purity?

The same bright light woke her up. Without opening her eyelashes, she began to remember the journey, when suddenly her heart skipped a beat, she opened her eyes wide. She remembered the young man whom her father had thrown out of the compartment. Before, she seemed to clearly remember his appearance, but now she has completely lost it. No matter how much she closed my eyes, she couldn't see him clearly. "He's also in this city!" This new thought, flashing like lightning, suddenly left in her soul both joy, and excitement, and calmness. Bagila was even surprised that until now she had never thought about her strange companion, had never thought about him.

There was a sound of unanimous laughter in the living room, the laughter was blocked by the loud voice of her father, then Maliks dropped the dishes in the kitchen, which shattered to smithereens. "She's drunk, right? It's strange, why does she drink on a par with men?!"

Bagila again began to think with pleasure about the unwanted companion and realised that those sitting in the living room had completely forgotten about the injustice they had done towards the stranger, that they would never remember him. Turgat, this flattering fox, ready to please, despite being requested by Bagila, did not find the stranger, and the papers remained with her. She sighed.

"Interesting!" she wondered. "Why am I thinking about him? Why should I think about him? And why am sitting here and getting worked up over him? For what? Because they forgot about him? Why should anyone remember him? After all, he was not put off the train, but was simply transferred to another compartment. All this is long behind me, no one remembers anything, only I... He probably forgot everything himself, but I still blame myself..." This consideration, which at first seemed like a whole revelation, somehow smoothed out the embarrassment for her father and then completely led to the conclusion that there is no reason to worry about a stranger and generally think about him. But, having already decided that this was the way it was, and that this guy did not deserve much thought, and even more so an experience, she felt a feeling of pity for him rise from the very depths of her soul. Something was clearly wrong with her. For the umpteenth time, her heart was restless. Oh my god, what is this?! She doesn't even know his name, but god, he just doesn't leave her head...

The door opened, and Malika's voice rung out, she called Bagila to sit at the dinner table. Bagila did not want anything to do with feasting, but keeping up appearances, she involuntarily stood up from her seat.

It was as if they had never seen her. As soon as Bagila appeared at the door, everyone except Karatai and Sargel fell silent and stared at her. They could not and did not try to hide their admiration.

For some reason, Turgat jumped up from his seat, accidentally poking his elbow at the plate that stood on the very edge of the table, turning the salad over on to the floor. Trying to pick up the fork that fell behind him, he carelessly bent down and buried his forehead in the thick cream of the cake melted by the heat. Realising that he should not show himself in this state, he disappeared under the table, allegedly in search of a fork. But he could not sit under the table until morning, he had to get out into the light of day, and he got out with the damned fork. At the same moment, a friendly ruthless laughter burst out.

Turgat hurried to the bathroom. The state of Karatai, who experienced acute jealousy because all attention was switched to his daughter, was saved by the collected laughter. And yet, he felt in his heart that Turgat's awkwardness was caused not just by a careless movement... Having felt it, he understood, in such a big city as Almaty, difficulties will arise in front of a beautiful girl, and it will be impossible to defeat them with mind alone. And his heart was sad and sorrowful.

Two days later, Karatai went home. They escorted him to the airport. When there was less than an hour left before the plane's departure, Karatai sent his men to register his ticket, and Malika and Bagel to get newspapers and magazines. He himself was alone with Sargel.

"I want you and Malika to support Bagila. You know what kind of city this is..."

"Of course," Sargel said, making an instant serious face.

"Bagila is the most capable among my children. But she, I think, is too headstrong. She won't mind your advice. Raise her like your own daughter."

"What are you talking about, Kara! You don't have to mention it! We are not strangers; how can I not consider her as a daughter!"

"Thank you, Sarga, I have nothing more to say. How about you, how are you doing?"

"Not bad, we live on the sly," he cleared his throat and looked down at the same time.

"What are you suddenly embarrassed about? Speak, do not be shy," Karatai remarked in a velvety voice.

"This winter... I had to defend my doctoral thesis..."

"Are you writing it?"

"It's written. All is ready."

"Oh, congratulations!"

"It's too early for congratulations. The thing is…" Sargel began and wanting to capture all of Karatai's attention, sharply raised his voice, "some of my colleagues are trying to harm me as much as they can."

"Why?"

"Because they don't want me to become a doctor. And you understand, they have learned many subtle dirty tricks, and so you won't guess where they'll kick you from. They call higher-ups and slander me with God knows what, they spread rumours that I am, they say, an ignoramus... They have no limits and say all sorts of nasty things. And some have filed a complaint against me. Can you imagine?! On me! Complaints! One scoundrel wrote that I drove my wife to death! Another accused me of marrying a young one. They're all loafers. Why do they care about my personal life? And what if I married a seventy-year-old? Then they'll will write a complaint that he has taken an old woman as his wife. And then, what does all this have to do with science, with my doctoral dissertation?"

Sargel spoke angrily, weightily, like a public prose-cutor, believing that he left no doubt in Karatai that he was right.

"I heard that such a fuss happens among scientists," Karatai remarked cautiously with a smile.

When they reached the end of the square in front of the airport, they turned back.

"It happens!" Sargel repeated sarcastically. "Yes, we have a fierce struggle going on, my friend. Outwardly they smile, but in fact they are ready to break me into pieces."

"And how are you defending yourself?"

"I don't know… What can I do? There is only one God, and I am alone…"

Karatai was silent. He knew very well every fad in the biography of his relative. He would really like to believe in his honesty, or at least helplessness, "God is one, and I am alone…" Yes, but that isn't so. After all, three or four years ago, Sargel got into some kind of trouble, he wrote complaints about someone, but the facts were not confirmed - not a single one - and he almost lost his position. "Do you remember?" Karatai wanted to say but restrained himself – he left his daughter to this man. Yes, Sargel is not the most crystal-clear person in this world and Karatai had something to say to him, but family ties involuntarily forced him to help his relative, to take an active part in his life.

"Is there anything I can help you with?" Karatai asked, not wanting to drag out this unpleasant conversation for him.

"I don't even know..." Sargel knew everything perfectly, but he dragged on, afraid that the conversation would lose its practical focus.

"Maybe you can do something, party organisations have great opportunities..."

Karatai smiled lightly and looked Sargel straight in the face. "Oh, and my relative sure is cunning," he thought, lowering his eyes so as not to give himself away, "How dashingly he sneaks up on me! It's like he doesn't know anything, but everyone knows who I am. And where does this attitude of his even come from? We're not all made from honey, but knowing that he tries it anyway, it's just scary."

They once again walked around the area with slow steps.

"Why did you have to wait until the last minute to tell me? You see, I'm leaving right now," Karatai said, feeling that Surge was waiting for an answer. "I'm sorry, I should have said this yesterday. Besides, I don't know who to contact with this question. Where will my protection be? At the academy or at the university?"

"In the university."

"Who do you need to talk to?"

For both Sargel and Karatai, the most painful part of the conversation began.

Sargel knew very well who Karatai should talk to, and besides, he was quite sure that Karatai knew these necessary people, and therefore he was angry that he was forcing him to say names aloud. And Karatai perfectly understood what Sargel was thinking at that moment. His comrade, with whom Karatai studied at the institute, was transferred seven to eight months ago to a responsible position in the Ministry of Higher Education. In principle, it didn't cost him anything to push Sargel to become a doctor, but Karatai was already painfully disgusted not only to go to him, but even to think about how he would go to ask, he would have to explain everything that Sargel told him so viciously...

"All right, Sarga," he said, sighing imperceptibly. "I'll talk."

"With whom?"

"There is a friend. You know... I haven't asked him for anything yet. It's going to be uncomfortable, of course, but it's whatever. The republican party debate will be held next month. That's when I'll go for it."

Sargel, as imperceptibly as Karatai, sighed, but was relieved, dropping a heavy burden from his shoulders. Hearing "there is a friend", he understood everything. Sargel knew who Karatai was talking about and who he would contact. This man was quite enough for Sargel to become a doctor, even if the entire scientific council is against him. His chest was filled with joy, the world shone in every colour. He felt like a master in this radiant world, stepping firmly, crushing all obstacles in his way.

"Sarga…"

Sargel turned around in an instant, seeing Karatai's face, marked by unchanging restraint and calmness, he began to listen intently.

"I learned that your sons lived in the room that they gave to Bagila. Make it so that on my next visit I can see portraits of your children and their mother. I don't think you need to explain what I mean by that. You'll understand. I'll tell Malika as well."

Karatai's words sincerely moved Sargel. He was pleased that, whilst busy with fun, table conversations and general attention, his brother still managed to notice the emptiness in the house, that he remembers his sons.

When they once again reached the end of the square and turned back, the announcer announced the beginning of the boarding…

Bagila became a student at the Faculty of History.

It is not clear why, but she was not happy when she read her name on the list of those enrolled in the history department. On the contrary, when she saw the girl weeping bitterly at the bulletin board, she experienced a quiet sadness.

"Three years… My God, three years!" the girl muttered, shedding tears. "How can I possibly go back to the village? No, I will not go back, I'd rather die than go back!"

It turns out that she came to enrol for two years in a row and each time she missed one mark. This year she missed half a mark. Bagila did not know whether she entered the university herself or it happened thanks to her father's brother. In fact, she did well in her exams. "Maybe I got in the way of this girl," she thought. "She's suffering so much, but I got into the university without any worries."

She also saw how another snub-nosed black-haired girl was delighted with her admission, clapping her hands loudly, like a child. She failed miserably in her history exam. The next time, when she came to take a foreign language, Bagila saw her name among those who took it, she could not believe her eyes. And today, having become a student, the swarthy girl did not know what to do with herself in joy. Bagila instantly hated this snub-nosed woman terribly. Trembling all over, as if a piece of ice had fallen on her heart, she angrily moved forward. She took out a kopeck piece from a small black purse and went into a pay phone booth. She slowly dialled six numbers.

"Hello! Lika, it's me, Bagila."

Malika liked being called that. She came up with this name for herself recently, removing the first two letters from the real one. "Lika". Brief and affectionate, Bagila liked it, because the hostess's invention eliminated traditional addresses, such as "tate" and "zheneshe".

Malika's frightened voice came from the phone:

"What happened? What happened?"

"I got in."

"Oh! You scared me! I thought you were in trouble... You sound kind of down? Aren't you glad that you got in?"

"I am glad..."

"Who could possibly be glad sounding like that? Oh, my little swallow. Run home now, while I call Sar."

"Call who?!"

"Sar. That's what I call Sargel."

"Ah! Okay, I'm going."

Leaving the booth, she walked slowly to the taxi stop. Malika has a strange habit of changing people's names. She does not call all her friends the way she calls them, but they do not take offence at her, on the contrary, they seem to be even satisfied. Bagila thought that one day it would be her turn. "Sar," she chuckled. "Wow!" Bagila, having imagined Sargel, tried to mentally address him, but immediately discovered the complete inconsistency of this word with the appearance and essence of Sargel, and almost burst out laughing at the top of her voice.

On this day, the three of them went to Medeo to sit in a restaurant. Sargel felt himself the main hero of the occasion, he was in particularly high spirits, not hiding that he played a major role in Bagila's admission to the university. And to his wife, and to Bagila, he was unusually attentive, spoke softly with the waiters, behaved intrusively correctly, trying his best to show how cultured he was.

They settled down near the window. Malika opened the blue velvet curtains, and the peaks of the mountains, trimmed with blue spruce forests, turned out to be so close it seemed: that you could stretch out your hand and you will prick yourself on cold hard needles. In Almaty, which lay far below, it was already night in the valley, but here the sun was still reflected in the high mountain glaciers. In the west, the sky was crystal clear, and the sunset was ablaze with scarlet light. A giant mudflow protection dam, having crossed two rocks with its steel shoulders, formed after a super-powerful directed explosion, was a shaky wall that protected millions of lives from the elements of the mountains, in the white-stone city. The dam has already settled down and is overgrown with high-mountain alpine grass. Above it, in the open expanse of the blue sky, mountains silently stood, bound by eternal ice. At the base of the dam, a ring of searchlights glittered on the bare ice field of the Medeo high-mountain skating rink.

The sun, meanwhile, rolled over the ridges, and darkness immediately thickened. The wind, cooled in the snow, flowed down into the gorge, swept in cold waves and stroked faces tired of the city heat.

"We are strange people, we don't appreciate our native nature," Malika said, without taking her eyes off this powerful, wild and proud beauty.

"Recently, our rector (Malika studied in absentia at the Institute of National Economy) was in Switzerland.

And he said that there is no corner in the world that could compare in beauty to our Medeo."

"That's pretty likely," Sargel agreed graciously with his wife, and suddenly tensed up all over. "Hmm... Where did you hear about this?"

Malika straightened up, her eyes cold.

"There was a meeting, Sar," she said, slurring every word while trying not to alert Bagila. "With the students at the institute!"

Sargel gave a short nod, his Adam's apple twitching as if he had swallowed a piece of ice, and the round mound went up and down his throat like a piston.

After that, while the waiter brought and set the champagne, they sat in silence. Bagila felt uncomfortable from this tense nervous silence, she didn't know where to put her hands, she touched the fork for no reason, moved the wine glass along the tablecloth and straightened her hair now and then, afraid to look at Sargel and Malika.

"Do you have any chocolates?" Malika asked the waiter.

"We have Pushkin's Tales."

"Bring one bar... And ice cream."

"One moment," the undersized guy, bowing too obsequiously, left whilst stepping slowly.

"I don't like waiters, specifically men," Malika said, opening champagne in a business-like way.

"And in the West, they don't like waitresses..." Replied Sargel.

"That's not true! That's all hearsay," Malika fiercely disagreed unexpectedly, waving her husband away as if he had said something monstrously stupid. "From the very beginning, nature divided duties between women and men. Then we ourselves mixed everything up so that now you can't figure what people are really supposed to do."

It can be seen that the champagne was warm, as soon as the wire on the cork moved away, it rushed out of the bottle with force. Malika could not hold the cork, and the champagne gushed from the neck into the face of Sargel, who, not wanting to argue with his wife, stared demonstratively nonchalantly out the window. He sobbed convulsively and began to sneeze like a cat bathed in water.

"Sar, I'm sorry, I didn't mean it," Malika said with sincere pity, trying to wipe her husband's face. Even after that, Sargel did not leave the heights of gentlemanly endurance, to which he exalted himself at the very beginning of the evening. He picked up the napkin with which Malika rubbed his face, dried his eyes and neck from the foam and said:

"Well, after that, how can we not love the waiter?"

For Malika, who decided that the evening was irreparably ruined, her husband's expression made a very special impression. It seems that for the first time in her life she looked at him with warmth.

The waiter brought chocolate and ice cream.

"Well, you can start your favourite dish," Malika said, looking at the girl with a smile.

Bagila really enjoyed the ice cream, but then she saw how one of the four young people sitting at the table near the entrance was staring in her direction. The guy was lean, high cheekbones, with shoulder-length hair. Just like Chingachgook. Taking another spoonful of ice cream, she looked at him... The guy smiled at her.

"Lika, that guy over there... he's not taking his eyes off me. I'm uncomfortable…" Bagila whispered.

"Which one?"

"Near the entrance, the long-haired one."

"I'm not surprised, let's see, let's see! Ah, the one with his chin in his palm?"

"Yes."

"Don't look at him, otherwise he'll think that you like him too, and then he won't leave you alone. Always do like this: just roll your eyes and he's gone. Especially if it's an artist or a sculptor, in general, anyone from that group."

"How do you know?

"Well, they're always the first to let go of their beard and hair.

"Why?"

"I do not know. Everyone goes crazy in their own way."

The orchestra struck out something from the repertoire of "Bony M". The bearded fellow, who had worked hard to look like Roussos, seemed to be longing for his drum during the day, for, hanging his head to one side, he began to walk with might and main with his sticks. The ringing of brass cymbals drowned out the entire orchestra, and, except for the drum, all other instruments were barely audible.

Malika looked at the drummer with displeasure and dislike. After her first failed marriage to a drummer, she couldn't stand the profession.

The dancing began. Bagila was amazed that none of the young people could really dance, everyone just twitched to the beat of the music. The orchestra members, as if pleased that they could instil such demonic excitement in people, tried their best.

A very young girl in a short black skirt danced surrounded by three guys. Her blond hair, falling wildly down her narrow back, beautifully set off her pale white face, sparkling golden under the bright light of the chandeliers. She did not jump like the others but instead, danced with skill. A light black jacket with a lace jabot emphasised her beauty. The scarlet plump lips were half open in a smile, behind them one could see wet shiny matte teeth. It was as if she didn't dance, but showed everyone how beautiful she was, how slim and young. The girl rapidly spun to the beat of the music, and a whirlwind of air, scattering a short skirt, revealed pink panties for a moment. The entire restaurant was staring at her, especially the men, who did not care about the music of their feast, and even more so their wives. Malika noticed that all the men of the restaurant were on the same face, and stealthily looked at Sargel. The piston that was stuck in his throat was moving from top to bottom faster than usual.

Malika jumped. "That's disgusting," she thought sarcastically, unexpectedly exposing her husband. "Look at what you desired before. You have a wife who is also sixteen years younger than you, and in the no way worse than that girl. And despite that, your Adam's apple twitches. No shame, no conscience!"

"Sir, your salad is cold," she said, specifically emphasising the last word as soon as the music had stopped.

Sargel, like a child rushing after an outstretched toy, abruptly turned to the table and, grabbing a fork, pounced on the salad.

"What licentiousness," he said, putting a piece of tomato in his mouth. "And where are that girl's parents? I do not believe that normal mothers should raise girls such as her."

"Is that the very thought that worries you?"

"What else can bother me?" he asked proudly, trying not to show that the girl's legs were in front of his eyes.

Malika felt it but did not pester her husband.

At this time, the waiter who was serving the table of long-haired men came up to them and took two bars of chocolate off his tray.

"From your guests," he smiled. "Those guys at the

table over there got these for you. See? And this is a note. To you!" He put a piece of paper folded in half in front of Bagila and left.

Sargel's eyes darted from the waiter to Malika, from Malika to Bagila. He did not know how to act at this insulting moment. Conscience and anger raged in him at the same time. The veins in his temples bulged.

Sargel immediately invited a waiter, put the gifts on the tray with his own hands and ordered them to be taken away, pointing his finger at the young people. He could not come to his senses for a long time, every now and then he swallowed from anger, cracked his fingers, terribly cracking his joints. Malika actually supported Sargel in his act, but she regretted the piece of paper, she wanted to know what was written there.

"But still," she began in a low voice, confident that she would not offend her husband, "you should have read what they wrote there. It wouldn't have been anything that bad…"

"We know what's written there! First, she reads it, then they get to know each other just like that, and then…"

"I get it, I get it, alright, I'll be quiet. I don't know why you're still fuming. You don't know anything about women. They are a hundred times more restrained than men."

"Sure, I know how restrained you can be…"

"Come on now, don't be like that! Not a single wise

man would tell you he fully understands a woman. Not a single one, and they will continue to not understand!"

"We-will-fig-ure-it-out!" said Sargel in syllables, for he was full of bile.

Malika decided not to retreat from her positions.

"Are you talking about the women you know?"

Sargel flew into a rage. He could no longer speak, only choked from an excess of words, proudly threw back his head, pursed his lips and froze in deathly silence.

The waiter served hot food.

"Hey, boy, bring us some champagne!" Malika said authoritatively, obviously to spite her husband.

"One moment!"

"Who will drink it?" Sargel shot his wife with his eyes.

"I will."

It was the end. Sargel's strength was waning. As if asking God for help, he stared at the distant spurs of Alatau. Nevertheless, on reflection, he realised that if something went wrong, if tonight is ruined, then that rumour about him will reach the ears of Karatai... Sargel sighed softly and took the fork.

"Why are they like this," thought Bagila. "How can somebody live like this? They are already at a breaking point, and there are still years ahead. If you cling to every word like this... Why did Malika talk about women, who are they, these women? What does Sargel have to do with them, and most importantly, why did he boil over? Why did he nearly burst out of anger."

Bagila remembered her mother, a quiet, unfailingly affectionate woman. She always paid attention to the mood of her children and her husband, she built her personal life in full accordance with the prosperity of her native hearth, thinking first and foremost, about the health of her family and so that evil would not enter the house. She also studied at an institute, knew no worse than others about the endless joys and sorrows of this life. But she always knew how to endure, knew how to wait. Bagila remembered - she was then either in the second or third grade - when her father worked at the state farm as the chief agronomist, there was a severe drought for two years in a row and he was removed from his post because the farm did not fulfil their tasks. He was in no way able to explain to his superiors and higher authorities that he was not to blame for this, that such a difficult situation had fallen not on one of their state farms, but on the entire district and even on the entire region, that he personally spared no effort in order to at least somehow - fix things. Even the responsible workers who visited their house knew her father well, they did not undertake to intercede for him, although they said that the trouble was not Karatai's fault, and that the agronomists of the region could be removed from work, but it would still not rain. It was the most terrible time for Karatai as he had just started to get on his feet, this was his first roadblock. Yes, people are different, and a friendship started at a good moment should be tested. Yesterday's friends did not only fail to stand up for him, they behaved as if they had never known Karatai, and this completely broke him. He was very worried, tried to leave his native places and settle somewhere on the banks of the Syr Darya. Though it was only his wife, Gainikamal, who restrained him, reminded him of his worth, and as befits a man, he must endure the hardships that had fallen before him. "There will always be work for the hands. Though you might not be in charge, you can still work as a simple agronomist, even as an ordinary shepherd. You won't be lost," she soothed him, cooling his fury. And she advised him how not to burn out in vain and strain his nerves in vain, she told him to go and see the first head of the region. Karatai, after weighing all the pros and cons, decided to follow Gainikamal's advice. "Indeed, what others did not understand, maybe he will understand? What am I doing here sitting on the couch? That way I won't achieve anything."

He did as his wife told him to. The first secretary of the regional party committee understood him correctly. He listened, paused and only said: "We'll see. You will be informed of everything." A week later, Karatai was reinstated in his former position.

And then eventually, the drought receded, his mood improved, and the state farm exceeded in their tasks by one and a half times. This completely invigorated up Karatai. He, more than ever, believed in his strength and capabilities. And then the next year the farm was lucky. At the regional party meeting, the same secretary praised Karatai for his skill and efficiency. The next year, in the spring, he rose to director of the state farm. Three years later he became the second secretary of the district party committee, and then the first.

During all these ups and downs, Gainikamal stayed the same, she did not droop and did not become proud, did not get angry at her husband's unnecessary words, that were said in moments of bitterness, "Well, how can you say such a thing!" she would exclaim, after patiently listening to him to the end. Calmness, Gainikamal's sound understanding imperceptibly calmed Karatai, it forced him to think seriously and control himself. And he could not help but feel that behind the wife's unchanging calmness there was a hidden warmth, and not just concerns about her family hearth or silent obedience to her husband, that she really cared for those who she loved. It also seemed to Karatai that he always understood her, and he tried never to raise his voice to his wife, not to say loud, stupid words that could hurt a person's soul. "Perhaps this is love," Bagila said to herself, becoming an adult.

Sargel and Malika, barely touching the hot food, pushed the plates to the middle of the table. It turns out that Bagila did not even notice how the champagne was opened, how they had already drunk a glass of wine. Did they really pour and drink each glass by themselves?!

Again, Bagila felt superfluous. Occasionally they turned to her, but only for the sake of decency, without any attention and joy to the event. It even began to seem to her that it was she who caused the quarrel between the spouses. In addition, the recent gift from the unfamiliar guys, the note brought disgrace on to her, it made her blush in front of her relatives. Maybe Sargel understands all this in his own way, that is, very badly, maybe he looks at her and his wife from completely different positions, it is quite possible.

Bagila suddenly felt completely alone. And these mountains, and the roaring river, and the skating rink, shining under the bright beams of spotlights, and the noisy city with its restless scurrying inhabitants, the student life that awaits ahead, this restaurant and it's reckless music, even the inflated Sargel and Malika - all this is somehow inexplicably moved away, became cold and flat. There was no person before whom she could open up, lean on their shoulder, count on, without sinning before her conscience. There, at home, she never felt such loneliness, although the life she led was not always arranged and smooth. Even when one evening at dinner, her younger brother read aloud the "Love Letter" (it was called that) written to her by a classmate, she did not experience despair and pain, she only tried to convince everyone that she did not know who wrote it. As she hoped, her father did not scold her, on the contrary, he besieged his son, who was in the fifth grade, put him in a corner, and he shed tears there for a long time.

After this uproar in the house, Bagila roused the whole class the next day. She finally found the one who was "in love". It turned out to be a lazy overgrown boy who ate corn in class and flicked the remaining hard grains at nearby girls. In his letter, he claimed that he would steal Bagila for himself. "If I am lucky to get on a saddle with you, then my father will not catch up to us with his car," he wrote. The boy's parents were called. They turned out to be livestock breeders, they came when the meeting had already begun. The boy's father silently listened to all the accusations against his son and, hearing that he wrote such a letter to the daughter of the district leader, looked at his child with furious eyes.

"Oh, you fool, did you eat donkey brains!" he shouted, pulling a horse whip from behind his top. "I'll scratch the skin on your back! You idiot, now I'll show you...!"

The people around them laughed in unison. The meeting has lost all meaning. Nevertheless, a protocol was drawn up, one copy of which was strictly handed over to the boy's parents.

Now, with some kind of self-pity, she realised that two years ago she was just an unintelligent girl, during that time she has matured a lot, and now ten years of school life, flying quickly and irrevocably, have become only a fleeting memory. And while she thought about this bygone sweet time of her life, the feeling of loneliness penetrated even deeper into her heart and responded with acute longing.

Suddenly, the image of the lost girl who stood weeping next to the lists appeared before her eyes. "How can I possibly go back to the village? No, I will not go back! Never!" Her sobbing voice came through clearly. And then the snub-nosed dark-haired girl appeared, bouncing in joy, and then hurriedly leaving, waving her handbag about. And then the already indistinct appearance of an unfamiliar person from the train surfaced in her memory. She remembered well only his cold eyes, his biting look, but she still felt how strongly her heart began to beat. Loneliness gradually began to dissolve, like fog under the blows of the morning wind. "Can it be," she asked herself, "that I really can't forget him? But why?" For the umpteenth time, succumbing to these thoughts, she did not notice how for some reason, she started looking around, as if she wanted to see someone... into frightening restlessness, feeling an unfamiliar tension and hot, pulsating chills all over the body. She did not want to admit it in any way, she was only surprised that lately - it was already impossible not to notice - she had developed that indifference towards him. "It's all nonsensical, made-up feelings," she thought at once, and, thinking so, she quickly agreed with this. And this was in fact the case, because today she did not think about him, and nothing happened to her. Yes, she didn't think about him, but... Lord, what a torment it is: for him to stubbornly surface in her mind, in some new, exciting light.

Sargel and Malika were busy with their quarrel and paid no attention to Bagila. It was actually a good thing, that they didn't know what she was thinking about at that moment...

They sat for another half an hour, then Sargel paid the waiter. They headed for the exit. The guys were still sitting there, and one of them was staring at Bagila. Sargel, showing with all his appearance that he was ready to repel any attempt on his ladies, stepped firmly and sedately.

When they came abreast of the ill-fated table, a long-haired man got up and blocked their way.

"Excuse me…" he addressed first to Malika, then turned his gaze to Bagila.

"Young man, let us pass!" Malika said sharply, showing how angry she was, unable to bear such monstrous bad manners.

"Excuse me, I must have lost my head a bit due to the wine..."

"Sir, if you don't want me to call the police, make way immediately," Sargel said, advancing on the guy. "What a disgrace!"

"I… did not mean to disgrace, I beg your pardon."

"I cannot forgive anyone who asks me for forgiveness," Sargel said, his eyes fixed on the top frame of the front door. "It doesn't matter, god bless you... Now get out of the way!"

"I didn't mean to offend you," the long-haired man blurted out, hurrying to say the necessary words before they left. As if hoping for feminine gentleness, he looked pleadingly at Malika. "I'm ashamed to stand like this... but how else could I have delayed you even for a minute. Don't be afraid of me... I don't know who this man is: your brother or father, but I'm not some kind of criminal, so I don't know why he'd threaten me with the police. I am a painter. In that note, I thanked you for appearing here, for the fact that there is such beauty in the world," he looked towards Bagila. "I have nothing more to say." He made way for them.

Malika was taken aback. She had no words, and, making a kind face, as if making it clear that she believes him, Malika passed by. Her soul felt warm, good, and she was ashamed that at first she was harsh with the young man, and nevertheless she noticed that the guy thoroughly touched Sargel with an abandoned phrase: "I don't know who this man is: your brother or father."

"My god, it's impossible to get some decent rest in Almaty," he muttered, angry. "Has everyone gone crazy, just drinking and dancing? A decent person has nowhere to sit! Wherever you go, they stick like oil, those 'artists!' Well, he should just stick to his brushing and pencilling! Let him draw mountains, stones, bushes for me, even turtles, what do I care about that!"

He walked away saying this, talking to himself, until he reached the taxi stop. And even in the car, he continued to mutter, warming himself up. When they arrived at the house, Sargel was already completely heated.

As soon as they entered the apartment, his blood pressure rose, and he went to bed. Let him feel bad, Malika was glad that her husband had finally closed his mouth.

Karatai, it turns out, sent a congratulatory telegram. It was shown to Malika by her 'sister' when they, after putting Sargel to bed, sat down in the kitchen to drink tea. Every time Bagila saw Malika's 'sister', an excruciatingly sharp pity arose in her. As a child, while playing on the street, she was hit by a car and was left without an arm and leg. Her neck was contorted by the terrible blow. The left leg, below the knee, passed into a prosthesis covered with a black stocking, and the right arm, bent at the elbow, froze on a sunken stomach. She never wore a dress or a skirt. To hide her misfortune, she wore trousers. In order not to catch the gazes of the people around her, she went to bed earlier than everyone else and got up later than everyone else. According to Malika, the girl was not really her sister, not even a close relative to her, but they were connected by some kind of distant relationship, and only at the request of her father, who lives in the village, Malika persuaded Sargel to take the girl to their house.

"Mance, didn't anyone call us while we were gone?" Malika asked as she poured jam into her tea. The girl's name was Mancia, Malika also shortened her name.

"Someone did..."

"Who?"

"I don't know. A man was asking for you."

"What's his voice like?"

She shrugged.

"Ordinary..."

"Well, high or low?"

"Low, thick. Like the actors!"

"Is that so!" Malika laughed out loud. "Did you do everything I told you? Are you ready for your class?"

"I did everything. I'm ready."

"Then call Karatai's apartment. I will chat with him before going to bed, he is due for good news."

Mancia silently nodded and went into the corridor, to the telephone, tapping her prosthesis like a wooden hammer.

"When does she finish?" Bagila just asked.

"She's only in her second year. We go to the same institute. God, I wish I had finished sooner! I can't look at her, so I try to send her away on business. She is probably offended by this, but my heart, it breaks for her..." She sighed softly. Suddenly, she quickly looked at Bagila and said: "You are very beautiful! For any woman, the real torment is to be next to you. Women don't like you. Except me!" She laughed a little chuckle. "If I were a man, I would definitely marry you. Only this is the misfortune of being the husband of a beautiful woman. You will live your entire life plagued by jealousy."

"Uncle Sargel, from what I can tell, is very jealous of you?"

"Yes, he is ready to die. He even gets jealous when I watch the TV. The trouble is that he does not have Majnun's pure jealousy, from the poem, but instead, some kind of petty, evil one. Sometimes it's so sickening, you just want to put a noose around your head."

Bagila almost asked her, "Do you love him?" But she said nothing, thinking that it was too early for her to talk about that, and that they would have many nights and days ahead when they would sit like this alone. Bagila was silent not only for this reason, but she also already knew that Malika does not truly love Sargel, their relationship is determined only by marital duties, they are completely different people in character, age, and they have nothing in common, especially their love for each other.

She only said:

"I feel guilty if he gets sick."

"Don't worry, he would have found a reason to get angry anyway. Each time we return home offended with each other. As soon as someone pays attention to me, his blood pressure immediately rises. So, you just have to stay away from jealous suitors. Oh yeah, that guy, I'm talking about the artist, I liked him. He turned out to be completely different then I imagined at the beginning. I love people who are open about what they think. Among these there are many honest ones, they do not live with cunningness and deceitfulness. Do you want to listen to music?"

"Sure."

"Let's go."

They left the kitchen.

"Mance," Malika called loudly. "Mance, how are you?"

"I asked for a negotiation. They said to wait."

"If we don't hear, call us, okay?"

"Of course," Mancia's voice sounded sad.

It seems that Malika understood a lot about pop music. The shelves were full of tapes and records of popular singers and ensembles. She pressed the "intimate" key on the stereo "Melody-103" and put on the record of Iovanna. Then they listened to Edita Piekha.

"I like them both," she said, reclining in her chair. "They touch my soul. They sing with feeling. In general, I don't give a damn about their voices, as long as they're sincere..."

They were silent again for a long time, listening to the music. The slow smooth melody helped to daydream; it carried them away to distant beautiful lands. The quiet house was full of prosperity, a cool evening slumbered outside the windows, it was so pleasant to sit in complete carelessness, calmly, thoughtlessly. Bagila was surprised by Malika's character. The hostess did not go to her husband to find out how he was feeling, did not look to see if her children were sleeping, did not ask if they were fed.

"Maybe she just trusts Mancia," thought Bagila.

"Eh!" Malika sighed. "Humans are interesting creatures! They are born, they grow and then they die! That's their whole life. They hurry, they strive for something, they wait, they hope for fate to bless them. And if it doesn't, they wait as long as they can, but if they crack, even once, they give up and don't get anything. And then they cry and obey, and they get used to it, lowering their heads. Years pass, they flounder, and they do not see: their lives slowly going out, like a flickering flame. They start getting old. And then, it's the end. You know, I feel so sorry for the old people, I myself do not want to grow old. I fear old age more than death. One old woman lived in our old apartment, probably in her youth she relied on her husband or children, you know the kind, one of those who hasn't worked a day in her life, and now, she's unhappy, she receives only twenty-nine rubles a month in pension. Just think, twenty-nine rubles! What can she do with that? Even if you spend one ruble a day, it won't be enough for a whole month. One day I ask her: "Where are your children?" and she just waves her hand. They had all dispersed, here and there. And they forgot their old woman. When we moved, she cried... She often came to us to talk, reminiscing about her past life, about her youth. I now visit her in my spare time. She is so conscientious, she does not even take gifts, she gets offended. I'm only able to bring meat and sugar during holidays or on the birthdays of her children. And then you know, recently… she started drinking. Probably from loneliness. It worries me, you see… Oh, how I do not want to grow old! You turn all grey, hunch over and be of no use to anyone. And I think I'm getting old… you know why? Because I started to feel that no one needed me. Perhaps only to my children, and even then, because they are children, and I am their mother. Little children… And then who else? My husband? Only as a woman. If I die, nothing will change in the world, the children will cry and stop, and when they grow up, they will forget. In return, another woman, just like me, will appear in this house. Compared to us, men are much happier. What, isn't it true? Imagine yourself in their place. Here, take me for example… When Sar dies, I will remain single, for whom will I marry with two children, who will need me? Therefore, one must live without thinking, without going into these subtleties, then at least sometimes, it will be easier on your soul."

Bagila was scared. She did not know that a person was destined to think about this sooner or later, more-over, during the month and a half that she lived in this house, Malika opened her soul for the first time, and there was nothing good in her. The radiogram, clicking, fell silent. Bagila was about to turn the record over, but Malika shook her head to stop her.

"We'd better lie down. They'll probably connect with Karatai any second now."

"Lika…" Bagila playfully twirled the record on her

finger.

"Yes?" Malika opened her eyes wide, big as those of a camel.

"These Pop chirpings don't mesh well with your soul. Personally, I think Chopin's ballads are more suitable for you."

Malika took these words surprisingly seriously.

"I knew you were smart," she said with an incomprehensible intonation. "Maybe, Chopin can do... I don't know what to listen to and what not to, what to read and what not to read. I was lucky, but not lucky enough to choose between Piekha and Chopin.

The phone rang loudly...

"Oh, it's your dad!" Malika exclaimed and rushed into the corridor.

A whole month passed since Karatai's arrival in Almaty, and finally Sargel was invited by the rector.

"Hello, Sargel Saynovich!" The rector stood up, moved towards, extended his hand for a greeting. "Please, sit down!"

Sargel did not know the exact reason for this unexpected call, and therefore answered questions briefly and warily. The rector rarely invited him to his place.

"How is your work?"

"Not bad," Sargel managed to pull off something that resembled a smile. "We're working hard."

"How is your relationship with the department?"

He was taken aback, not expecting that such a question could be asked directly, and even by the rector. Sargel had been waiting for this moment for a long time, hoping that someday he would get a chance to explain to the rector what kind of people, his colleagues in the department, the ones that had "dug a hole for him," are. But in a matter of seconds, it was difficult to gather the thoughts together, and he thought, is it necessary to open up to the rector? Maybe, him asking that question, was just a coincidence...

"It's different for everyone... The work is in progress," Sargel replied, hoping he was being ambiguous. "Thank you for being interested in my life. I often only see you on the move, but I never managed to talk to you..."

"Yes, unfortunately, that's the way it is... There is no time for everything, we are slaves of time," the rector laughed. "If I'm not mistaken, we've been working together for almost ten years, and to be honest, we don't know each other very well. Hello, goodbye, that's all we say and then continue with our own lives. So, I decided to find some time today and talk to you properly. In two days, I'm flying to Berlin, where there is an international symposium of biologists..."

"Yes, I heard, I heard! I wish you a great journey!"

"How are you doing with your dissertation?"

"I've finished it. I am currently preparing my abstract."

"That's good... Although I'm not a historian, I think I can appreciate your work." He laughed again.

Sargel was well aware of the rector's habit of rising from his seat and smoothing his hair when he thought he was joking or hearing a well-aimed word. And this time the rector followed his habit, as if glad he was able to tell that joke.

"Thank you," Sargel said, trying not to show he had taken the hint, but his voice quivered with joy, and the blush that flared on his face betrayed him completely. "Although I am a historian, I always read your work, trying to understand them. Sometimes I want to express my admiration to you, but I'm afraid that they may be misunderstand..." He glanced at the rector's face. Yes, he was right. The chief outwardly remained imperturbable, but only outwardly, Sargel easily noticed that the rector was pleased with his words. "Personally, I am surprised how you find time for science and use your time so efficiently. Please, do not take my words as flattery... As for the situation at the department... with your permission, I will tell you my opinions about this, about the relationship of teachers, what they think about their leadership, after your arrival from Berlin. You should not waste time on this now, since you are already on your way, why get upset over trifles?"

"That's right," the rector was pleased. "We'll talk again when I get back from the symposium. More frankly and thoroughly, okay?"

"Of course!"

"See you then."

"Bless you…" Sargel said, respectfully rising from his seat, said goodbye to him with his hand. "If you don't mind, I'll take you to the airport."

"Oh, don't remind me. No matter how much I fly, I'm always afraid. It's also good that there are a lot of friends seeing off, helps me forget about the fear. Indeed, true friends will save you from all troubles."

"That's great! I'll be at the airport then!"

Sargel left the rector's office in a great mood. He walked past the pulpit and into the street. Walking along the square, decorated with fountains, he thought about the details of the meeting for about an hour. "Is he disposed towards me?" he asked himself, once again recalling to the smallest detail in the behaviour of the rector, his look, his movements, his words. "Why not? But why, then, has he not brought me closer to him until now? Why has he never asked about my work before? Even more, after that complaint, he seemed to dislike me…"

Sargel thought of Karatai.

"So, it turns out he talked to his friend. Well done, Karatai! A true relative! Well, now try to compete with Sargel," he muttered, pleased with himself. "Who now from this accursed pulpit will dare to reproach me? And I don't think I talked so badly with him," he continued to rejoice for himself. "How he, the fool, melted from praise! He believed that I was reading his nonsense. What else am I missing! Damn it, what would I have done if he asked the title of even one of his works? Oh whatever, why would he be asking me that anyway? A person who is weak to flattery does not need specific praise." Sargel chuckled. He remembered the expression of some playwright: "Ears, greedy for flattery, but with talent it's tight..." Having ventured such a bold and biting assessment of the rector, he felt how pleasant it was to think badly about his boss, but he caught himself in time, even looked with caution sideways, afraid that someone might read his mind. Suddenly, Sargel remembered that the rector had asked his opinion about the teachers. "Why does he need it? For what? Or maybe..." His heart began to beat again, but he did not even dare to mentally say it: "Or maybe he wants to hand over the reins of the department to me?"

So, enjoying these thoughts and at the same time being frightened by them, he stood for a long time at the fountain. "As soon as Karatai arrives, we will have to invite him to visit, with that person from the ministry and the rector."

It was an excellent idea. Sargel sighed lightly and returned to the university. Now he saw these semi-dark departments, bare bluish walls, scurrying students and teachers in a completely different way. There were always a lot of people around him, but now he had one significant difference from them: all these people became lower and weaker than him. That is why he crossed the threshold of the pulpit - for the first time in many years - boldly and proudly.

"Lika!"

Sargel howled in good spirits. He sat in a comfortable armchair and enjoyed watching the colour TV.

"Lika, come here, 'In the World of Animals" is starting."

"I know, I know, I'm coming!" She bathed the children, put on fresh linen for them and approached her husband. "It's early, isn't it? Wow, another fifteen minutes!" she remarked, looking at the wall clock.

"No, they are behind."

"Perhaps, though maybe your watch is going a little fast Sar," Malika jokingly said, not wanting to disturb Sargel's mood.

She warmly dressed the children after the bath, arranged them in armchairs in front of the TV, continuing to wipe the younger's forelock with a dry towel. Sargel sat behind them, and as Malika bent down, the top button of her robe came undone, revealing her breasts. His body was hotly pierced by an electric current. In fact, he did not like it when a woman had such freedom in her clothes, he never got tired of criticising those who wore light, short dresses. When lying down in bed, he did not see the female body, he considered that looking at his naked other half was dirty. Now he accidentally stumbled upon his wife's snow-white breasts, and it is not clear why he wanted to look again... And - it was completely unbelievable - inside him slowly, carefully, but still, a warm, intense wave arose. Against his custom, he did not make comments to his wife. "What is it with me?" he thought. "No, it cannot be. A man at fifty is still strong. Maybe it's because I didn't really look at Malika like this before, or is it true that a man over fifty gains new strength?" The last thought calmed him and gladdened him. He returned to his high spirits again.

"Where is Bagila? Why is she not with us?"

She's probably reading. From morning to evening, she does not tear himself away from books," said Malika. "Stuff like that can lead to psychosis."

"On the contrary, it is excellent quality. One can only rejoice."

"A woman, buried in papers, forgets that she is a woman. And when she forgets about it, she disappears as a person! Bagila!"

The girl didn't answer. Malika, slapping her slippers, went to her room and opened the door. And there she was. Bagila, resting her cheek on her hand, buried herself in the book. She had managed to read half of their library. Once again, Malika involuntarily admired the girl... Oh god, how she would like to have the same light, playful strand of silky hair that falls on her right eyebrow, as the girl before her. Like a doll, she thought. "Wow, not a single flaw!"

"Sur," Malika said, not noticing how the abbreviated name appeared on her tongue and surprised at the unexpected find.

Bagila looked up from her book with a smile.

"Did you decide to call me that?"

"What? Sur... This is from the word 'picture'. In addition, Kuprin has a story called "Olga Sur". Anyway, let's go see 'In the World of Animals.' This show is 100% true."

"You are always busy searching for the truth." Bagila got up from the table. "Will Mancia watch?"

"She is doesn't like this program; she generally doesn't like the TV. She likes to be alone. She says that when she is alone, she can present a story much more interesting than the plot of multi-episode television films. So, she has her own TV in her head."

Bagila did not want to leave the room, but fearing to offend Malika, she followed her. Stepping over the threshold of the room, Bagila froze, as if pierced by a current.

"What happened? What?" Malika was worried. Bagila was silent.

"Sur, I ask, what is the matter with you?"

Malika screamed in fright. From this cry, the girl came to her senses. With wild fear in her eyes, she looked towards the TV. On the screen, a man was finishing talking, something about literature. Nobody in the room listened to him.

"It's him!" she whispered. "It's him! God, I can't forget him."

"Who?! Who is it?" Sargel stood nearby with a glass of water, looking at Bagila in amazement, Malika gave her a drink.

"We need to put her to bed!" Sargel decided. Malika took her back to the room and laid her on the sofa.

"Do you have any pain?" she asked, looking at the girl with pity.

Bagila shook her head. He reappeared before her eyes, the impudent young man from the train. All this time, she unconsciously searched for him and then she saw him... Again, the same cold face, cold look, and again only for a few moments...! "What was he talking about? What did he say?" How she regretted not being able to listen to him, to see him closely. She already believed that without much difficulty she could forget him, now her confidence crumbled to dust. Her heart was beating so desperately that Bagila realised that the "unpleasant passenger" had taken a firm place in her soul, and she could never forget him.

"Is this really how it will be?" She thought, returning for the thousandth time to the question that had tormented her for so long. "It turns out that I... No, it can't be, did I really fall in love at first sight?"

"We need to call an ambulance. Your face is pale."

"No, I'm fine now."

"Have you ever been like this before?"

"No…"

Lie down, I'll give you a cold compress. Malika left. Sargel paced restlessly in the kitchen.

"Karatai's father had heart problems, and that finished him off. It turns out that it is true that the disease is inherited…" he panicked, clasping his hands. "Such a young girl, it's a pity! I wouldn't even wish a heart attack on my enemy. Well, it's kind of parasite, you can never be cured of it!

"Enough," Malika told him. "Who asks you to show your knowledge in medicine?! This is well known without you."

Malika, squeezing the water out of the gauze, hurried into Bagila's room.

"I don't need anything," said the girl, completely coming to her senses. "I don't have any pain, and in general I have never been sick."

Malika carefully looked into her clear, calm eyes and said softly:

"If my woman's intuition does not deceive me, something special has affected you? Tell the truth, what's the matter?"

Bagila stared unblinkingly at Malika's smiling face, bending over her, her eyes full of kindness and pity. And she read in those eyes: "Tell me, I love you very much, trust me as you trust yourself. I am your true friend." Bagila was moved.

"Lika," she whispered softly, "I love you…"

Hearing this unexpected confession, Malika laughed in her silvery voice.

"So you decided to scare me?"

Bagila smiled.

"Of course not..."

"So, what's the deal? What's wrong with you?"

"I... Lika, you won't laugh, will you?

"What am I, a fool, or something, to laugh at a serious matter?

"Just a while ago, on TV, I saw him..."

"On TV? Whom?"

"That guy..."

Malika puffed out her lips, looking dumbfoundedly at Bagila.

"That guy? Who is he?"

"I do not know..."

"Well, Sur," she drawled, spreading her arms. "Either you still haven't come to your senses, or I've started to lose my mind! I can't understand anything!"

Bagila told her how it all happened...

"Hmm... It looks like you're in love with him," Malika concluded after a thoughtful pause. "Don't worry, it happens. Especially at your age."

"I don't think it depends on age. I don't just like him..."

"Oh, poor Sur!" Malika sighed jokingly. "It turns out that you, before you even reached us, fell in love with him... And I..." She laughed again. "I thought you had everything ahead of you. Yes, me too..."

"How so? Have you lost everything?"

"No, but – half of myself, because, having lived to this age, I loved several times, but not longer than a month and a half. Though, I didn't come across mine when travelling... but you, you lost your cool the first time. Love can be compared to a disease. It also has ups and downs, and most importantly, it is curable and incurable. Oh, my Sur, how happy this unforgettable person must be! If I were in his place... probably my heart would break. So, what are we going to do?"

"I do not know..."

"You know how to fall in love, but you don't know what to do, right?!" Malika pinched her nose like a little girl, then, rising from the sofa, opened the door and called out, "Sar!" Bagila jumped in fright on the bed:

"Lika, what are you doing? What do you want to talk about with him?"

"Lie still, little doll," Malika said, stopping her with a movement of her head. "Now we will check what Sar knows about literature. Sar!"

Sargel was at that moment in the toilet. Apparently, having decided that something was wrong with Bagila, he fussed there, rattling his stand, and shouted in a hoarse voice: "What? Give me a minute!"

"You can stay there with complete pleasure. Sur feels fine! Tell me just who recently appeared on TV?"

Bagila, seeing that she couldn't stop Malika, sank

into a chair and covered her face with her hands.

"What is it?" asked Sargel, falling silent again.

"Well, it's necessary. I think I've seen him somewhere..."

"Where?"

"If I remembered, I wouldn't be asking you! I think he's the one that didn't pay me for the mare milk!"

"Jasyn Madiev."

"Is he talented?"

"Recently, he's become quite popular."

"Do you like him? I'm talking about his books."

"I don't read them. But the newspapers shout with each other about the fact that there isn't a more talented writer than him."

"Sar, congratulations! You got a five on the test! Especially in such a difficult situation." She closed the door and turned to Bagila: "Because he does not know about his works, it'd probably give him a two, but so far, his works are not of interest to us. Well, did you hear his first and last name?"

"God, what a shame! How can I look Sargel in the eye now!"

"Don't worry about it. How could he know why I asked about this writer. Anyway, we found out the main thing. Now it's not that hard to find him. We'll call the Writers' Union, and they'll give us his address and phone number. Well, shall we try?"

"For god's sake stop it! There is no need."

"Why? How are you going to find him?"

Malika paused, thought for a moment, and soon said nonchalantly:

"We'll see how it goes. Time will tell. Let's go watch TV."

"No, I'll still be here. I am ashamed to be in front of Sargel."

"Okay. You can sit with your "beloved" as long as you like."

"Li-ka!"

"Ciao!" She affectionately patted Bagila on the cheek and floated out of the room. "And I'll stay with my dear husband."

She uttered the last words cheerfully, but Bagila still caught the hidden bitterness in them.

"Jasyn," Bagila repeated to herself. "Jasyn Madiev. Jasyn… 'Lightning?!' Jasyn…! That's who he is!"

Bagila read two of his books. And she re-read it more than once, literally on the eve of leaving home, she again held them in her hands. To be honest, Bagila was surprised by his outlook on life, his deep understanding of life, the thoughts and feelings of his characters, and the high culture of writing. Newspapers lifted his name to the skies. She also read devastating articles, but they only rocked the waves of his popularity.

Today, his name and face combined for her. As soon as the program about animals ended, Malika looked into Bagila's room.

"Sur," she said, sitting down in the armchair next to the sofa. There was significance in her voice. "You shouldn't go through with this... I just called an actor. They appear to know each other well."

"Go through with what? Know who well?"

"Well, that's... You shouldn't fall in love with that man. He is a married man. He has two children."

Bagila froze, trying her best not to show that the news had an effect on her in the same way as the appearance of Jasyn on the TV screen.

"Lika," she cried ardently. "You... why do you think of me like that?! When did I say that I was in love with him? When? Why are you humiliating me…" She turned away, not hiding her offence, and fell face down into the pillow, shedding warm tears.

"Okay, okay! Don't worry like that. If I offended you, I'm sorry. Sur, don't be mad at me. It's my duty to tell you this because I'm worried... I don't know why, but when I think about you, I get scared. Maybe it's all rubbish on my part, maybe not. Well, forgive me!"

It was clear to see that Malika could not bear to look at Bagila crying, and she left her room.

"Just booked a call with Karatai," Sargel said. He was in a great mood.

Malika was scared.

"Why are you doing this? Don't talk about what happened, don't! She is perfectly healthy."

"It's not about that," Sargel said nonchalantly. "It's a

different matter. I want to talk about our business."

He did not dare to tell his wife about today's meeting with the rector: he was afraid that she would start gossiping and the meaning of their conversation would reach outsiders. Sargel did not trust his wife…

As soon as Malika left, Bagila closed herself off with the latch from the inside and gave way to tears. She did not hide the fact that she could not forget him and admit that she was "in love" with him! It was beyond her strength, her pride.

The last days of September passed by. The rain that had begun in the morning turned into snow, then again gave way to cold rain. The paved avenues and sidewalks were covered with dirt, leaves and all kinds of things. Almost a month has passed since Bagila and her fellow students went to work in agriculture. Sargel wanted to leave her in the city, and Malika supported him, fearing that Bagila would fall ill inadvertently, but the girl was eager to live away from the city.

Malika croaked; it was as Sargel had warned. Two days after leaving, Bagila suddenly developed a fever and fell ill, although the work was not that hard, they were just picking apples.

The young teacher Serbota, who brought them to the state farm, became alarmed and wanted to immediately send her back to Almaty, but Bagila flatly refused. For four days she lay in the state farm hotel, which was specially vacated for students.

For all four days Serbota never left her side. She was suggested to lie still, but Bagila, avoiding unnecessary words and suspicious glances of her fellow students, she went to work!

Serbota was energetic, single, and with all his energy he plunged into torments of love and arrived in Almaty completely emaciated.

Though it was very clear, that there was not a single guy on the course who did not fall in love with Bagila.

Under any pretext, four or five 'fans' were always around her, Serbota, as a teacher, could not be among them and, watching the lucky ones from afar, was tormented by jealousy. By nature, inclined to the exact sciences, he fell into a poetic mood of spiritual anguish and wrote lyric-philosophical letters to her.

Bagila did not answer these messages, but sent them to Malika so that she, reading them in her free time, could cheer herself up…

The sky was completely overlaid with heavy grey clouds and, apparently, the sun disappeared for a long time. The Karagachi trees, standing in a row on both sides of the road, having lost their yellowed leaves, dozed in the rain, were naked and dark. And the high-rise city houses looked sad, dull and grey. Lectures ended earlier than usual today. On the way home, Bagila turned into a record store, but not finding anything she liked, went outside and started hailing a taxi. Soon she managed to stop a car in which one passenger was sitting. She did not see his face. The girl gave her address.

"Get in, we're on our way," said the driver cheerfully. Bagila folded her umbrella and settled into the back seat.

"Are you going home or to a hostel?" asked the man sitting next to the driver without turning his head.

"Are you asking me?" Bagila was surprised.

"Who else! There is no one in the car except you."

"Why do you need to know that?"

"Do you like being rude?"

"See it however you like," said the girl in an unhappy voice.

"Should have figured! I expected a different answer from you, but you're no different from the others, are you?"

"Why should I be different?" Demanded Bagila, the man chuckled.

"It's whatever, I don't care. I just wanted you to be different. Where is your father, here or in the village?"

The stubbornness of a stranger, clinging like a tick, touched Bagila.

"You don't know my father, so what do you care about him?"

"Oh, I know him very well, and I know you."

"Driver! Sir! Stop the car," asked Bagila. "I'm getting out!"

"Keep driving," commanded the passenger in a confident cold voice. "By the way, did you get into university?"

Bagila was taken aback by this question and confused.

"How did you know…?"

"Well, I would tell you, but you said that you're getting out of the car. I'm well acquainted with you. I knew in advance that you would definitely enter the university?"

"Why?!"

"And you knew that very well. For you to get into a university is a technical matter…"

Bagila glared furiously at his stooped back, at the thick bristly hair lying on the collar of his coat, at the long-swollen earlobes.

"You seem to be very offended by life," she said, trying to offend him.

"That may very well be… By the way, before I forget, did you tear up the papers that I left in your compartment?"

Lightning flashed before her eyes. It felt as she had taken a blow to her body, even the blood in her veins for a moment froze. My God, how did she not immediately recognise his voice, his special intonation! The car, running squelching through the wet snow, suddenly seemed to dive into an inky dark tunnel. The light disappeared, and only after a while she again clearly saw his back, stone-tense. The one who tormented her for so long, who deprived her of peace and confidence in life, was sitting right in front of her, at arm's length. "It's fate!" Bagila involuntarily though to herself. "Who would have thought that we would meet like this, in a taxi, in the middle of a dirty street! Just like in the movies!"

"What's with the silence? You threw it away?" He half-turned and looked askance at her.

She begging to lose it! Again, that cold face, again the icy gaze, piercing like an arrow.

"No, I have it," Bagila whispered in a barely audible voice.

"Thanks for keeping them. There are some very important entries in those notes. I bet you aren't too interested in them, but I was very worried about losing them, when can I take these papers from you?"

Jasyn fixed his gaze on Bagila. Eyes that looked calm and straight, without hesitation, that pressed her to the seat.

"You're right, I don't need those papers for any-thing," Bagila suddenly blurted out, not controlling herself. "You can pick them up at any time. Where should I take them?"

Jasyn looked at the girl with surprise. There was a slight warmth in his cold, indifferent eyes.

"Thank you for your honesty. It may seem confusing to a stranger that I care so much for those slips of paper, but I've only told you the first reason, and the second is that I do not want even the insole of my shoes to remain in the hands of people I dislike."

The last words went through her like a twig soaked in salt. Looks like he was just a boor.

"Yes!" Exclaimed Bagila, seized with rage. "You are right, for us your writings are no more expensive than a rotten old insole. I might have accidentally bookmarked a page of my book with your nonsense!"

Anger made it difficult for her to breathe, and she began to crumple the umbrella in her hands, feeling the knitting needles bend under her fingers. She could not look at Jasyn, but all the same, she felt the bile emanating from him with her whole skin. "He sees that he pissed me off. He is provoking me up on purpose, so that I burst with anger, like a girl!"

"That's good," he said, turning to face her with a condescending smile. "I think you have lectures after dinner. Why how you are right now, you probably can't even tell me what kind class you're in, what floor, and so on. So, let's make a deal. Tomorrow I will find your class according to the schedule and we will meet during the break. In my opinion, it will not be difficult for you to take my nonsense with you. And if this is humiliating for you, pass it on through someone. I will come during the break after the first lecture. Deal?"

Bagila was silent. The sharp, imperious tone suppressed her, did not allow her to open her mouth. "If it's humiliating?! Wow, what delicacy!" Bagila already knew that after this meeting she would have to fight with herself all night, that both anger and affection for this person, who settled in her at the same time, and despite this fight, that heat would still prevail and she herself would bring him this paper. And while rage stood in her throat, even tears welled up in her eyes.

She stopped the taxi right outside the house, handed the driver a ruble, thinking that he would refuse if this tormentor wanted to pay for her, but he did not think to do so.

Without looking at the road, she quickly walked towards the house, forgetting to open her umbrella. She passed under a high arch, turned to the entrance, and then suddenly saw an embarrassed figure. "Who is it now?" she thought angrily.

"Bagila," they called out to her.

It was Serbota. He looked at her pleadingly, huddled in a wet, sagging cloak. It was obvious that he has been trampling around in the rain for a long time! Streams of water ran from the brim of the hat onto the damp, darkened shoulder straps of the cloak.

"Mr. Serbota is that you?!" the girl asked in astonishment as she stopped.

"Yes, it's me. I'm sorry I'm here..."

"Mr. Serbota, what's the matter with you! You're like a child, why are doing this?"

"You mean to tell me to go home?"

"No, but... It's awkward somehow... Uncle Sargel knows you well, if he sees that-"

"Let him."

"You don't care, what about me? Tomorrow will be a day..." Said Bagila, trying to get rid of him. "You'll catch a cold..."

"So what. If it's for you..."

"What's for me?" She looked at him, not knowing how to extricate herself. "What a shame... Go away, for god's sake, I beg you..."

"I'll call you later..."

"No... no! Listen... They can see everything from our windows. Listen... I have to get going now, all the best to you."

"Let's step aside..."

"You... if you don't want to offend me, then leave now..."

"I won't leave until you promise to spend next Sunday with me. I'm tired of waiting and being patient."

"Oh my god, how do I get away from him! What do I do?" She thought.

"Fine..."

"Are you saying it like that just to get rid of me?"

"Lord, what is the matter with you today...! I said fine, got it!"

"Thank you," Serbota blurted out. "You can go, and I'll just..."

Bagila quickly ran into the entrance, loudly slamming the door. She was finally left alone; she leaned her shoulder against the wall and closed her eyes. "One thing to another," Bagila whispered.

When she entered the apartment, Malika screamed in fear at the top of her voice, "What happened?" Bagila sank wearily into the chair by the door.

"I saw."

"Who?"

"Both of them."

"Wh-what?"

"I said both. One in a taxi, the other at the entrance."

Oh lord, seeing how ridiculous it all way, Bagila managed to form somewhat of a smile.

"Goodness, you won't rest until you drive me completely crazy. Speak more clearly!"

"Like, let me undress first," said Bagila, pulling off her wet clothes.

"Sur, you're... not drunk? Are you?"

"Lika, he can't stand me. Me and all of us..."

Everything that happened today, she laid out like a spirit.

"Lika," asked Bagila, looking at the ceiling, "Is all this nonsense really necessary in a woman's life?"

"This is just the beginning darling."

"Really?! In this case, all this must be endured, endured. Lika, I don't want to love anyone."

"It's not in your power, Sur... Love comes in without permission, it won't even consider how you feel."

"Did you love anyone?"

"I used to love..."

"I'm asking you seriously."

"Why should I lie, I'm telling the truth."

"And how did it all end?"

"You know with what... my marriage to your father's brother."

Bagila saw an undisguised bitter smile on her face.

"You... why did you marry Sar? After all, no one pulled you on a lasso. Well, who forced you against your will to go to the registry office?"

Malika, stretching in her chair, sighed deeply and crossed her arms over her chest, leaning forward with her whole body.

"Sur, this is a long and, moreover, nauseatingly boring conversation. It is not interesting to anyone, and first and foremost, to me. Sometimes I want to forget about my whole life. If I had such strength in my hands, I would throw everything that I have lived out of my head and live in anticipation of the next happy day. All this is such nonsense, my husband was a "composer", weak-willed men like him are no better than that tyrant Sargel, who killed his wife with his animalistic jealousy, tormenting me like rain slowly chiselling down a stone! Try to look at all this a little deeper. Millions of years have passed since life arose on earth. Of the life that follows after us, we know nothing. We came into this life with consciousness, thought, speech, the ability to understand sounds and colours, grief, joy. We come for a short time. We are in a hurry; we have a very short existence. So why did we even show up? In order to, having married a "composer", divorce him in three months? In order to distribute the deficit to men who, instead of masculine honour have a woman's desire to fill up the refrigerator? Or in order to become the wife of that half-wit Sargel?" She said the last words with anguish. "What! for this I was given life?!"

"Lika, but do you have any goal? Any dreams?"

"—I don't know, Sur... It's hard to put everything into one word. Until the last minute, I was waiting for some wonderful changes, new twists and turns. And then I got tired of waiting, all my dreams dried up, like grass on stones. Everything is clear, everything is simple. No secrets, no mysteries. In the morning I go to work, an hour break, dinner, sleep... This is how everything will go from day to day, for the rest of my life…!"

"Lika," exclaimed Bagila, "you should have become a writer or a traveller. You shouldn't have locked yourself in the store."

Malika suddenly laughed with a small chuckle and pressed Bagila's beautiful nose with her fingers.

"Your thoughts have become sharpened! What other questions do you have?"

"But you didn't answer any of the questions!"

"Another time, Sur. It's eleven now. I have to get up early tomorrow. Besides, if I talk to you for a long time, Sar will get jealous. God, he is jealous of me even when I'm watching TV or even sitting on a stool."

"So, he loves you with all his heart."

"Yes, of course, that's why he is jealous of me on a stool!" Covering her mouth with her hand, she laughed contemptuously. "Sometimes it seems to me that he came into this world only for jealousy..."

Bagila laughed along with her.

"Laughter suits you," Malika remarked. "Everything suits you. Well, okay: listen to music, read books, dream. In the end, you will leave this room either a wise woman or a mad woman. And one more thing... Sur, I don't want to interfere in your personal life. You have enough of your mind. But look, you are still very young, try, as far as possible, to stay free longer. You still have lots of time to wash the dishes for your husband."

Malika left.

Bagila looked at her bed, lying at its head, she saw the sheets that she had to take with her tomorrow, and quickly ran through them with her eyes. Now the words were clearer and more understandable than before. In addition, she heard Jasyn's low, coldish voice when she read them...

Putting the paper in her purse, she looked up at the ceiling. Then into the deer's glassy eyes. The heart fluttered again. Those eyes were very reminiscent of his eyes - sharp as an arrow, cold as a dagger, deep as a well in the sand. He was very close and very far. Scary and expensive.

She was hoping this lecture could last forever. And when there were a few minutes left until the end, it began to seem that the old bald teacher either was playing for time or was deliberately in a hurry to finish the classes as soon as possible. She had forgotten that there would be a call. She didn't care what the teacher said. For the entire hour and a half, she was looking for an answer to the question: "Do you take it out yourself or pass it on through someone?"

Bagila flinched as the bell rang. Thoughts shattered like glass falling on a stone floor.

Standing up, she hurried towards the exit. All doubts were easily dispelled. Everything was clear to her: she herself would give the sheet.

Bagila hurriedly followed the teacher and immediately saw Jasyn in the far corner of the corridor. He smoked, glancing at the auditorium door.

"Hello," he said, approaching Bagila. "Excuse me, what is your name?"

In an effort to show that she had not forgotten yesterday's insult, Bagila decided to silently hand over the paper and leave, but she did not succeed.

"Bagila," she answered with a tremble in her voice, and rushed frantically to look for the ill-fated pages in the book.

"Not the best name," he remarked. "It's viscous, like Almaty caramel."

"You... you impudent! What right do you have to talk to me like that?! You have no right." Bagila whispered all of this, fighting back tears.

"You're right this time." She slipped the sheets carelessly into his inside pocket. "Thank you! Now I can say goodbye for good thanks to this, but I want to tell you one other thing, don't be afraid, this has nothing to do with love or any of that nonsense. You seem to have enough boyfriends here without me."

He hit it on the spot again. Bagila's arched eyebrows quivered, and Jasyn understood everything without difficulty.

"I don't have time tonight," Bagila blurted out.

"In the evening? Lovers meet in the evening. You go out now. It's okay, without this lecture you won't become any more stupid. I'll be waiting downstairs. Near a pay phone."

Having said that, he turned and left. By the time Bagila came to, he had already descended the stairs to the lobby.

"Bagila, who was that?" asked the girl sitting next to her during the lectures.

"A Relative."

"That's not true," the fellow student intervened. "You don't know him! And I know who he is. Everyone knows him as Jasyn. I wanted to get an autograph, but I was afraid to break your trills!"

"Jasyn!" Roared the crowd of students." Wow! You

should have said right away! I didn't know he was so young?"

"And he has eyes! Like lightning!" Bagila's girlfriends even blushed from the thoughts.

A fellow student got into the conversation again:

"Jasyn is his pseudonym. Let her say his real name because they are relatives."

"What's his real name?" The girls shouted from all sides.

There was nowhere to retreat, since she said she was his relative, it was impossible not to know her real name.

"Zhylkaydar."

"Wow! Zhylkaydar! What a lousy name. Turns out he's just horse rider. Zhylkaydar Madiev! With such a name, one shouldn't be a writer, but a livestock specialist on a collective farm. But Jasyn - wow! That's a name that corresponds to a great writer who can strike like lightning!"

"Bagila, is he really your relative?"

"Yes."

"Why didn't you tell me? Introduce me, okay?"

"What great news! What treats are we getting to celebrate!" A lanky guy stuck his head through the crowd. His head was large, and his neck was long and thin. In the summer, when they wore only shirts, his head looked like a boxing glove, put on a stick. Hiding this flaw, in summer and winter, instead of a tie, he wore a nylon handkerchief around his neck.

"Oh, you'll get treats!" the girl smiled. "A glass of mango and a raisin pie!"

"I'll take it!" The guy hugged her.

"Oh, go away!" the girl said, pushing him away from her.

"Why do you want to get to know him anyway?" The guy did not let up. "Firstly, he is married, and secondly, he has two children."

"So what! For love, this isn't a barrier."

The bell rang. The students trudged into the auditorium. Bagila, not knowing what to do, stood in thought. A student grabbed her hand.

"Taklamakan is coming! Let's go to the classroom!"

The teacher who read the "History of the Ancient World" was named Taklamakan. He often used "so" in his speech, in addition, he had a monstrous bald head, and the students called him "Taklamakan Desert". It is not known when this nickname originated, but it was passed down from alumni to freshmen. Over time, the word "desert" disappeared and the nickname "Taklamakan" remained.

"Zhanat, can you bring me my purse!" Bagila turned to her friend.

She quickly flew into the auditorium.

"Are you coming back?"

"Yeah, in an hour."

"Are you going on a date with Jasyn?" Bagila winced.

"Don't worry, nothing wrong with that. Say hello

for me. I immediately realised that you are relatives the same way me and Alla Pugacheva are. Well, good luck! Disappear quickly, Taklamakan looms near!"

Bagila ducked into a nook in the corridor.

They settled down at the last table of a nearby cafe. Jasyn ordered coffee, lemonade, champagne and a chocolate bar. They didn't say a word while the waitress prepared the table. Jasyn opened the champagne and filled the glasses.

"For the return of my notes!" he raised his glass.

"I don't drink," she said without looking up.

"As you wish. Why did you go to the history department?" he asked, staring at her.

Bagila was taken aback by the unexpected question.

"Don't be shy," he reassured her with a smile. "I am used to speaking openly on any topic and advise you."

"To be frank," she said, trying not to look at Jasyn, "I regret that I met you after yesterday's incident. I can't forgive myself for sitting here..."

"What a miracle!" he exclaimed. "I guess I should be offended."

"Everyone has their own reasons. You insulted all of us. You didn't even consider me a person. I... I never heard such words, and I didn't think I would... I wanted to tell you that you insulted me greatly."

"You are more talkative today," said Jasyn, nonchalantly sipping champagne. "I must tell you that the conscience is not divided into large and small, moreover, it is not divided into male or female. The sorrow you feel is negligible, it's like the granddaughter to my insult... If I'm not mistaken, your father, he's the big boss?"

"Why do you need to know? Don't drag my father into the conversation. Or I'll leave..."

"It's easier for you, you can get up and leave of your own free will, but when they kicked me out, well, I think there is a difference."

She was confused. In front of the guy whom his father kicked out of the compartment, Bagila always felt guilty. In addition, this person turned out to be not just anyone, but the well-known Jasyn.

"Okay, let's not talk about it," he said. "We will not achieve the desired results if we arrange a trial of each other. So, why did you enter the history department?"

"I want to become a historian."

"Is your beauty really so necessary for a field such as history?"

"Hello, by the way, it's from my girlfriend..."

"Mm, what's she got to do with it?"

"I don't know... What connection did you find between history and human beauty? What does that have to do with it?"

Jasyn, bringing the glass to his mouth, stopped it, then put it back on the table.

"I'm starting to like you," he said, looking at her curiously. "I like the thoughts of a person more than their eyes."

"I know."

"How?"

"From your books, I even re-read the last two."

Jasyn stroked the rim of the glass with his fingertip and looked at the girl with undisguised interest, he was painfully ashamed of her every word.

"What else have you read?"

"Some other books, here and there..."

"You have a peculiar way of thinking. What were you yesterday... like an evil cat?"

"Because you... immediately began to be rude. You know, I spent the night thinking about what to do. I even cried."

"Why did you come today? I didn't really beg you, I didn't roll at your feet."

"To bring you your notes..."

"Is there another reason?"

"Are you waiting for me to say that I came here for you?"

Jasyn took a sip of champagne. Grabbed the cold coffee.

"Well, well, you are becoming dangerous!"

"Why did you invite me here? Or did you forget by any chance?"

"No. You know, I have a lot of things in my head about you. Now here I want to turn it all around, starting with our skirmish on the train... Then it will be the turn of the collar that is history, which you, without hesitation, fastened around your neck.

"What's so strange about me wanting to be a historian?"

"You ever heard of the breed of horses known as Akhalteke?"

"Well, let's..."

"Well, it is the most beautiful breed. Do you admit, that the Akhalteke horse needs to be collared? Personally, I can't imagine it!"

"And what kind of breed are you, since you decided to evaluate people through means of horse breeding?" Bagila laughed, feeling pleased that she had hooked Jasyn.

He was surprised not only by her beauty, but also by her strong, naturally courageous character, which she did not hide from people. Jasyn smiled.

"Yes," he said. "I am an Akhalteke! And you too..."

"I have an... aunt here, she calls me Sur. This is connected with Kuprin's story "Olga Sur" and something else... And now you're going to start calling me Akhalteke. It turns out that I have to say goodbye to my own name."

"Do not be offended by the Akhalteke. If I were god the almighty, I would create humans not from monkeys, but from the Akhalteke breed of horses."

"By the way, modern science has not fully confirmed the assertion that man originated from monkeys."

"That's irrelevant, the main thing is that we came from somewhere. According to our legends, we are created from the clay of a bird. Honestly, I would cross out all this and create people from Akhalteke."

"Then… what would we be like?"

They both introduced themselves as descendants of horses and laughed with pleasure.

"We would get used to it," said Jasyn with a smile. They began to laugh at the appearance of monkeys. "It all depends on habit. Do you think monkeys, if they are able to think, consider their life worse than ours? Yes, they should only rejoice that they did not become people... But we've deviated from the main topic..." He again switched to a strict tone. "I do not like well-fed people. Because the well-fed are always blind and deaf. Because they do not need art, the prospects of tomorrow, any changes in the world, digestion is more important for them. They need an apartment, a position, a personal car, and nothing else. They will go through life without feeling or experiencing anything and will leave life without noticing it. The most annoying thing is that the amount of such people hasn't decreased. There are those who, in order to rise higher, are ready to trample underfoot even the Koran, even Abai. I don't like being with people all the time. I'm afraid to meet a thoughtless look, a head full of thoughts about consumption. I tried to look at myself critically, I thought that I did not have the average relationships with people. Unfortunately, I was not mistaken. I do not belong with well-fed people. At first glance, I noticed that you are different from them… This is what I was going to tell you today. You still don't know how far you stand from the cheap crowd that sleeps and seeks to settle down somewhere warmer…"

Bagila listened with special attention to these strange words of Jasyn, in which revelation and despair sounded. Never before in her life had she met a person who would say things the way he did… And all this was not invented this very second, but, apparently, it took shape a long time ago. She remembered how long she had been looking for him from the moment he left the compartment with the angry flash of his eyes, how, going out into the street, she saw him in everyone she met. And now she is sitting next to him… But, how strange, until that moment, as soon as she remembered him, she lost her peace, her heart was torn out of her chest, and now, for some unknown reason, she was calm and even, as if nothing had happened. This was a new experience for her, an absolutely amazing feeling. It was not only just the attitude of a girl to a man, but a sincere craving for an intelligent, thinking person. The new feeling gradually subdued the first – the feeling restlessness and discomfort. She suddenly felt joy because her mood was determined, and she wanted to tell Jasyn what she thought about him before this meeting, how she hated him and realised quite clearly that she could no longer be without him. She wanted to drink a full glass of champagne so that her head would spin, and her thoughts would lose their sharpness.

They spent an hour in the cafe. The sky was cloudy, but the rain had stopped. The young birch trees growing near the cafe had not yet warmed up after yesterday's sleet and were freezing silently, without rustling their leaves. Two willows leaned over the empty pool, covering their concrete bottom with lancet leaves.

Wet leaves crunched underfoot. They walked in silence. Bagila, chilled after the warm hall of the cafe, turned up the collar of her coat, put her hands in her pockets. Walking where it was drier, she strictly watched that Jasyn did not get very close to her. Bagila only now noticed that they were the same height, as if cut by the same sword. In her eyes, this was Jasyn's only flaw, she preferred the girl in a relationship to be shorter, even the same height did not suit her. "My shoes prop me up," she thought, as if trying to justify Jasyn. "It's seven centimetres, so I'm below him. Great! After all, it's beautiful to be lower than a gentleman, this is a universal standard!" She smiled and stealthily glanced at Jasyn's shoes. And his shoes propped him up as well… No more than five centimetres, she decided. That's only two centimetres. "Well, whatever, I'm still below him. Wonderful," she even shrugged her shoulders. "What am I thinking about? What nonsense! I'm walking next to him, and there's nonsense in my head…"

"Do you have class?" Jasyn asked when they went

out along the alley of the park to the avenue.

She paused and answered cautiously:

"I don't want to go. I'm not in the mood for a lecture."

"Did meeting me have such a bad effect on you?"

"It's the opposite... I want to calmly think, but it's noisy there, like in a bazaar."

"If for each new thought you need to leave class, then... you will kicked out of university."

"No, no!" the girl laughed. "Don't be afraid!"

They walked rather quickly along a free street and did not notice how they ended up a block from Bagila's house.

"You notice," Bagila asked, slightly touching Jasyn with her shoulder. "Yesterday we managed to say a lot in a taxi, but today we were together for more than an hour and did not agree on anything. Why is that?!"

"You don't need to ask about it," Jasyn said, frowning his eyebrows. "That's what the heroines from sentimental stories say. The answer has been known for a long time."

"You don't like sentimental things?"

"I can't stand them."

"Interesting! And I thought..."

"Bagila," Jasyn stopped her. "Indeed, what a disgusting name, exactly the name of a cheap caramel. Did you say that your aunt calls you Sur?"

"Yes," she answered curtly, pouting her lips.

"Well, it's not perfect, but it's better than your actual name. I will also call you Sur. So, Sur, can't you just keep quiet!?"

Bagila blinked rapidly, and her face burned with fire. She felt so ashamed and hurt that for a moment she even forgot where she was.

"Come on now," he said impatiently, not looking at her. "Sometimes there is more sense in silence than in endless chatter. In any case, when people are silent, the illusion of understanding each other is created."

"People are silent when they are alone," she said passionately, ready to burst into tears.

"Wrong, absolutely not! In loneliness thoughts are vague, and when there is a person like you around, thoughts become stricter."

The words "like you" instantly knocked down the flame of rage, and Bagila's soul instantly subsided, like a kitten under a gentle hand. "He's thinking about me!" She exulted, losing her breath. "Sometimes he is soft, like a camel, and sometimes he beats like a twig. What an individual!"

They stopped at her house.

"Let's say goodbye. I asked you to stay with me for one hour," he looked at his watch, "but I took almost three hours from you. I beg your pardon." He handed her a business card. "Call me if you need to. Feel free to do so at any time. And one other thing... Let's tone down on this 'love' nonsense."

"You... your shameless! How dare you!"

"Sorry, but I noticed that you're treating me in a special way. Don't bother."

Bagila cried.

"You're so selfish! You like to mock, trample on the honour of a person! Go away. I don't want to see you."

"It is not for such a smart girl as you to shed tears, to say stupid things in a fit of rage. Everything has to be looked at sensibly. In the moment, these words of yours are useless."

"Get out! Goodbye."

"It never even crossed my mind that we would part like this. Don't be offended. I just said what I thought, and you decided that I'm trying to mock you. Though that just isn't true. Anyway, good luck!" Jasyn had already turned, took a few steps, but then stopped. "Tomorrow I'm flying abroad. I'm coming back in ten days."

"I don't care where you're going and for how long you'll be gone!" sobbed Bagila, stuffing her handkerchief into her purse. Noticing that Jasyn was not leaving, she took a step towards him. "Where are you flying to?"

Jasyn smiled softly. She saw warmth flicker in his cold eyes.

"To Cuba. Together with a delegation of writers."

"Have a safe journey…!"

"Thanks! Well then, should we say goodbye by hand?"

She gave him her hand and felt the warmth of his fingers. She held her palm in his palm, and it pierced

Jasyn's heart. He winced and withdrew his hand.

"See you later."

Bagila nodded. Jasyn quickly walked away. Turning around, he saw that she was looking after him.

She entered the apartment by opening the door with her key. In the living room, Oginsky's Polonaise blared at full power. It means Mancia is home. When left alone, she always listened to music, turning the radio on at full volume.

Bagila changed her shoes and went to her room. At the open doors of the living room, she froze in disbelief. Mancia, clasping a puppet in a sailor's uniform with her unbending left hand, danced waddling like a duck. Her eyes were closed, her head lay on the doll's shoulders, but Bagila knew that Mancia's neck was simply twisted. She took clumsy steps, not keeping up with the rhythm of the music, it was especially noticeable because the prosthesis tapped on the floor out of time. A thin bluish jacket and tight jeans only emphasised her ugliness. Bagila could no longer look at the poor woman and quickly went to her room. There, she threw her bag on the table, she felt a leaden weight on her heart.

After sitting idle in an armchair, she mechanically picked up a book, "Shadows in Paradise…" She re-marked… Even since it's purchase, Bagila had no idea who the author was. The book opened with a crack, as if it had dried on a shelf. Bagila flipped through the novel unaccountably, unsticking the pages. She did not want to read. The Polonaise was still playing in the living room. From the minute Bagila entered the house, Mancia put on a record for the third time. And so, the dancing with the sailor doll continued.

Soon the music stopped. Mancia could be heard putting the record into the envelope, turning off the radiogram and, loudly banging her prosthesis, moved into the kitchen. In the corridor she stopped, the wooden knocking stopped. A switch clicked by the hanger. Then Mancia went back. Bagila hurriedly buried herself in the book. When the door of her room banged open, she shuddered and looked up...

Mancia looked at her with hatred. Bagila waited in horror...

"Well, did you see enough of how I enjoy myself?" Mancia whistled, spraying white saliva.

"Mance..."

"Shut up! Don't call me Mance! You have no right to this!"

"I just came," Bagila whispered, not knowing how to extinguish her tantrum.

"You're lying! Well, show me how many pages you've read." She ran up to Bagila with surprising speed and snatched the book out of her hands.

"Only the first page! So, you were following me!" She threw the book on the table.

"I swear I just got here! I don't understand what

you're talking about…" Bagila babbled.

"You're lying! I touched your coat, it's already warm, here's your bag, it's warm too! You came a long time ago and watched me... You... You laughed at me, yes, you laughed! You're just pretending to read! Mrs. Gorgeous! All beauties like you are cunning and two-faced! I do not believe you! I hate you!"

Bagila was silent, trembling at every one of Mancia's movement. She did not begin to talk about the fact that she behaved quietly only because she was afraid to disturb her mood - now it was impossible to explain anything to Mancia.

Mancia, fixing her furious gaze on Bagila, stood for a while, then, biting her lip until it bled, she left, slamming the door loudly.

Bagila breathed a sigh of relief and picked up the book again, even though she knew she wouldn't read it. From the page, Mancia's eyes full of rage and anger looked at her.

She closed the book.

On Sunday, Bagila had to involuntarily fulfil her promise to Serbota, and Bagila spent two hours with him.

"Lika," she exclaimed cheerfully, entering the apartment.

Malika was feeding the children in the kitchen. Hearing Bagila, she nimbly jumped down from her chair and hurried to meet her.

"Why so fast? What, you quarrelled?"

"Oh, Li-ka-a!" Bagila laughed, shaking her head. "How stupid men are! Do you know what he said to me?!" She giggled a little. Malika, warning her, moved her chin towards Sargel's office. Bagila, as if saying "Oh, I completely forgot about him," covered her mouth with her palm. On tiptoe, they went to Bagila's room.

"And what did he say?" Malika, with a curiosity inherent in a woman, bombarded Bagila with questions, as soon as they closed the door behind them.

"We didn't say a single word until we reached the park and then we sat in silence in the restaurant. Only on the way back, once we reached the house, he suddenly says: 'Let's get married, Bagila.'" She giggled again, and Malika began to laugh with her. "Oh, so funny, my stomach hurts. He teaches at the university, writes his Ph.D. thesis, and he himself is like a child! Even schoolchildren don't talk like that anymore! Where did he manage to preserve himself so well? Hmm, 'let's get married!' Oh wow, he made me laugh!"

"Though, what's wrong with that?" Malika remarked. "He's not the worst option. And if we talk about his naivety, then, quite possibly, it comes from his purity. Don't you think so?"

"Maybe, but... he's in the thick of life. He hears, sees, reads and, despite this, does not even know how to talk to a girl. And then how can you say, "let's get married" on the first date?!"

"And what was your answer?"

"Well, what could I really say? I said he was late, I said I'll go and ask permission from my fiancé. I don't know how these words came out…? I also laughed… Look, is it still worth it?"

Malika cautiously pulled back the curtain.

"Is he wearing a hat and a white coat?"

"Yes."

"He's leaving."

"Phew! God bless. I was afraid that he would stand there until morning."

Malika, lowering the curtain, sighed softly:

"Still, it's a pity that this happens!"

"If it's such a pity, I can get him to come back. Just need to give him a shout…"

They laughed at the same time. Their laughter was interrupted by a loud doorbell. Malika, as if asking: "Who's at the door?!", looked inquiringly at Bagila and went to open it. Sargel seemed to be equally interested in the sound, hands behind his back as he paced between the kitchen and the office door. As soon as Malika appeared in the corridor, he opened the front door.

On the threshold stood a young man, no more than twenty years old.

"Hello!" he said, bewildered, encountering inquiring glances.

Sargel nodded in greeting and pursed his lips.

"Who are you looking for?"

"I don't know," the guy was completely embarrassed. "There was… one person … my friend, who sent me to come to you."

"You? To us?! Interesting," Sargel was surprised, looking first at Malika, then at the guy. Distrust of his wife had already flared up in him for a long time. "Who is this friend of yours?"

"A painter. A good artist…"

"So what does a good artist want with us? Does he want to paint our portraits?"

The guy, apparently, realised that he did not have enough endurance to continue this conversation, leaned an object folded into white paper against the wall.

"He wanted to give you this picture. I don't think I got the wrong address… I'm sorry to bother you," and the man ran down the stairs without waiting for an answer.

Sargel and Malika looked at each other inquisitively. Malik perfectly understood the look of her husband, in which there was nothing new, except for stupid jealousy.

"As if the things before weren't enough, now we have some idiots sending us gifts to our own home. Well, let's open it, let's see what's inside," said Sargel, arrogantly putting his hands behind his back.

Malika went up to the picture and began to untie the packaging.

From the way the nylon thread was skilfully tied, how clean the drawing paper was, how carefully the picture was wrapped, she realised that the unfamiliar artist did all this with a special disposition. Before them stood a large portrait in a gilded frame, dazzlingly shining in the electric light. It was a portrait of a beauty, painted with oil paints. At the bottom right were the artist's initials "E. I."

Sargel and Malika, not hiding their admiration, involuntarily held their breaths and looked at the picture. Deep, black eyes, like a moonless night, eyebrows raised, as if asking questions that were born in the figure's curly, charming head. And the look... This is how a person who has made a discovery looks. And to that person, this discovery, as if in the very next moment, is about to be told through the childish tender lips, the opening gleaming with dense snow-white teeth.

This is what the artist saw.

"It's... Bagel!" Sargel yelled, recoiling from the portrait. A blush broke out on his lean, high-cheeked face, and he looked dumbfounded at Malika.

"Did you find out just now?"

"I thought it was you..."

"Oh, what a disappointment that must be! Trust me, I would die of happiness if someone drew me like this..."

Sargel noticed how excited his wife was.

"Ha!" He looked furiously at Malika with sudden anger. "Then let's invite this artist! This is the same guy who sent you half a litre at the restaurant on Medeo!

Let's find him, and for good money he will paint you in any form."

"He can't draw me like this…"

"What do mean 'like this?!' What kind of portrait must he paint for you to die of happiness?

Malika looked up at her husband for a moment.

"Like this one, exactly like this!"

"But that's Bagila…!"

The words of her husband, uttered with obvious mockery, inflamed whirlwinds of rage in Malika's chest, but trying not to give herself away, she called on all of her self-control to help.

"Sar," she said with a tremble in her voice, almost a growl. "Go and check on the children for a moment. Go, for god's sake…"

She realised too late that the last words should not have been spoken. Sargel immediately went after them and yelped in a thin voice:

"Why for god's sake?"

Malika, not finding worthy words, pathetically answered:

"They've been sitting alone for a long time…"

"What's the point in saying for god's sake?"

"Sar, for god's sake, go to the children," Malika repeated softly, never taking her eyes off the portrait of Bagila. "Go on… you keep forgetting that pettiness wears out the nerves and ages a person prematurely."

Old age… It was a blow to the most fragile place. It

had nothing to do with him yet, but Sargel was terribly furious when he heard the words "ages" from the lips of his wife, as if he was some "old man." What Malika had said left him speechless and drove back down the words he was about to splash on his wife's head. He left, raising his head high, stepping as importantly as a crane. Once he reached the kitchen threshold he turned around and said, shaking his chin:

"This daub better be gone before I wake up tomorrow!" And slammed the door.

The imperious voice of her husband, who firmly believed in his power, the impudent slamming of the door brought Malika to her limit. She stood for a while, mastering herself, then resolutely followed her husband. Sargel, who did not expect such courage from his wife, looked at her with dazed eyes.

"Sar," Malik said clearly, determined to keep herself under control at all costs. "You know, I don't allow myself to argue with you in front of the children, but now I have to put you in your place, because everyone heard how you yelled at me. Okay, I'm not going to burst like a soap bubble because of this. But remember, you shouldn't interfere in Bagila's personal affairs. She is not your daughter. In addition, she did not ask the artist to draw this portrait. So I'm not going to carry out your 'order!' Got it! I understand that you can't bear to hear such words, but you've got no other choice this time."

Sargel put down the knife with which he had cut

the children's pie with frightening slowness, timidly, without taking his eyes off Malika's face, he stood up and straightened up as heavily as if he had a heavy load on his shoulders.

"Who do you think you are?! You…" he muttered under his breath through his teeth.

"Yes, it's all me, you're not mistaken! But that portrait should not be thrown away, it's just short-sighted decision. Imagine what Bagila will think," Malika said more gently, wishing, on the one hand, for reconciliation with Sargel, who stood frozen as a corpse, and on the other, a little wary of him.

Sargel didn't say a word. Finally, after being frozen for what felt an eternity, life reappeared in his eyes. He put his hands behind his back and walked out. "Now his heart will seize again," thought Malika with anguish. "Maybe I shouldn't have pushed so hard? Oh, to hell with him, it's his own fault!" She separated the children, who were grappling over some trifle.

"If you're full, go to bed," she called out. "You won't be able to wake up tomorrow. Come on, get up from the table!" After wiping the children's hands and mouths, she sent them to their rooms. "Lie down and no talking, alright!"

Seemingly understanding the mood of their mother, the children, pouting, silently began to undress.

Malika went to Bagila.

"Did you quarrel again?" Bagila asked, raising her

head from her book.

"Of course, what else can I do with him!"

"Is it because of me again?"

"No, because of the artist."

"Because of what artist…? Ah, did he remember our trip to Medeo."

Malika smiled softly: "Let's go into the corridor."

Bagila, catching her slippers on the way, went after Malika.

Seeing the portrait, she did not understand at first, and then arched an eyebrow. She raised her hands to her cheeks and her face flushed.

"So, do you recognise the face? Unlike Sar, you figured it out quickly. He thought that it was me," Malika said, watching how Bagila was stunned looking first at the portrait, then at her.

Bagila came to her senses with difficulty.

"I don't think it's anything special…" she said uncertainly and with a tremor in her voice.

"How is it nothing special?"

"He saw me once and immediately drew me... Shame on him, right Lika?"

"You didn't go to pose for him. Or did you..."

"What are you saying?!"

"Then there is nothing to be ashamed of. If anything, this is not your portrait, this is an artist's fantasy based on his fleeting memories! It's nobody's fault that you're stunningly beautiful. And your beauty is not your personal property, other people should also admire it. God created beauty for this... What do you know, maybe in a hundred years the portrait will be considered a masterpiece. Our descendants will know that in the seventies of the twentieth century a beautiful and intelligent creature lived on this earth."

Bagila could not understand whether Malika was joking or serious, but her confusion dissipated.

"That's why Sar and I didn't get along for a bit," Malika touched the painting with an imperceptible movement. "He is against portraits as a genre in fine art." She laughed through her teeth. "Where shall we hang it? In your room?

"No."

"Okay. We'll think of something tomorrow. It's good that he drew you. If I had been painted, Sar would have hung me instead of the picture."

"Lika, you don't have to argue with him all the time."

"Oh! I can see you're starting to feel kindred feelings."

"I just feel sorry for him."

"Oh my, aren't you merciful! Fine, today he's had enough on his mind, last thing he wants is to hear more from us. Take the portrait and put it in your room. If you don't want to look at it, cover it with a towel." Malika laughed again and, pushing Bagila towards her room, went to Sargel's bedroom.

Sargel, without changing the position he had taken in the kitchen, stood by the unmade bed and looked out the window. Malika, as if nothing had happened, went to her bed and began to get ready for bed. Only then did Sargel turn his whole body towards her.

His eyes were still bulging, as if he had not moved his eyelashes since that moment. Malika saw that he began to move, but pretended that she did not care at all, and got ready to sleep. Sargel moved around the bedroom like a clock pendulum, she did not hear when he started his next sermon.

"From the day of the creation of the world, after a man and a woman drank the cup of marital unity, they were obliged to live in peace and harmony under one frame, at one common hearth. Even if the moment comes to prove something, it is not done with their throat, not with anger and rage, otherwise a crack appears in the family, which becomes deeper in the future. I do not believe in equality and democracy between spouses, which is talked a lot about at the present time. The family should be dominated by one of the spouses. And where this is not the case, the family ceases to be a family. Equality and democracy are not grounds for the coexistence of representatives of the two genera, it can break like a glass vessel that has fallen on a stone, due to random contradictions, minor mistakes. Therefore, dear Malika," he continued, pacing back and forth and raising his voice at the word 'dear,' "there is no place for democracy in this house. That anger on your part, a violent invasion of me in front of the children, and even with a sharp jerking of the door, this is a mockery of the spouse. A woman in any situation must respect a man. Perhaps some women consider themselves smarter than their husbands, but, unfortunately, this wisdom is not confirmed by anything. On the contrary, if a woman is conscientious, she respects her husband, does not affect his honour..."

"Sar," Malika said as she settled under the cold blanket, "are you done with your lecture?"

"No," he didn't even look at his wife. "And I'm not lecturing you. Whether this conversation ends or not is up to you. If you understood everything I said correctly, then I'm done."

"I understood everything." Sargel stopped walking, looked at his wife. "There is more anger in your voice than resignation. I do not believe you."

"Don't make me grow old, Sar," Malika said in a velvety voice.

Sargel's head twitched slightly, and he stared at his wife for a long time.

"That's right," he began a new tirade. "All men..."

"Drop it, for god's sake!" Malika asked angrily. "Who are these 'men' you're talking about? Men, men, men. What do you care about men?"

Sargel looked at her in furious surprise. Hypocrisy, together with anger, warmed the blood in his sclerotic veins, and his eyes nearly popped out of their sockets. In the words "What do you care about men?" he heard "you are not a man." Besides, the wife said it calmly and weightily. So that means she had been thinking about it for a long time, and then the opportunity arose to say it out loud. And she said it... Coming to this conclusion, Sargel almost burned himself in his own fire, for the fire burned with might and main in him. In addition, his wife picked up a book in her hands with indifference, without being nervous at all, she opened the right page and, without paying attention to it, began to read! He choked with rage. Looking at his wife's calm, carefree face, at her half-exposed white breasts and sloping shoulders, he realised for the first time with all clarity that he could never defeat her, that no matter how much they grappled, defeat would always await him. And behind this painful confession, another fact slipped through... He is not a worthy match for this woman. He cannot offer anything worthy of her sharp mind and young strong body, which wants to live not in peace, but with passion. Such thoughts, which first appeared in his head, began to awaken new feelings in the recesses of his chicken breast. It seems that for no reason at all, he suddenly remembered his dead wife. But she was much softer and more submissive than this woman. She silently listened to him and did not read Dumas novels at night. Yes, she would not have swaggered, not puffed up arrogantly, like this one... She would have been silent as usual, and this is much better than the behaviour of this one... "So, she considers herself superior to me, it turns out that to her, I'm no different to a wall, a chair. I scream, I get nervous, I prove something. What for?! What can I prove to her? The thing is, I'm dependent on her, and she doesn't care. That's the point!"

These arguments were unbearable for Sargel, choking with hatred and impotence, not wanting to stay near her, he went out into the corridor with an unfortunate air. "But it's such a trifle!" he thought, standing in front of the window. "It'd be shameful to tell others that someone else's portrait painted by some artist! Would be the reason for our divorce? For our family to split. It'd be a delight to our enemies. That we are so petty we stumble over any kind of nonsense? Damn it, we are strangers to each other...! And if I die?" He winced at the thought. "Will she even cry? No, she doesn't care!"

He saw his first wife again. Then his two adult children. His two sons who live on their own.

Suddenly he realised that everyone had cooled off towards him a long time ago: the children singing in the next room, Malika... All of them can live without him, none of them need him, and if he dies, no one will be especially worried, no one will ask God to bring him back to this earth.

And his friends and comrades are the same. And Karatai is no better, he only pretends to be worried about him.

"Why is everything like this? What is the reason for this? Where are these people who cannot live without each other? Where are they? Why do I not see others dying because of the death of another?"

He felt like an orphan who did not have and will never have a single close person in the world. "What is it? Why is it so dark in my eyes? Is it from old age? Perhaps this is how old age enters the human body. With this darkness, with such thoughts... Will the rest of my life really go like this?!"

Sargel again began to delve into his bitter thoughts, but quickly came to his senses. "It will not work," he said to someone with malicious gloating. "There is no use in these arguments. You have to be persistent. Yes... persistent... "

Feeling decisive, he breathed a sigh of relief and went to check on the children, from the children's bedroom, undressing as he went, he moved towards Malika. She slept, forgetting to put out the night lamp, dropping her book on the floor.

He glanced over the body of his wife, showing through under the covers, and, to his happiness, did not pay attention to the fact that his male desire did not even stir in him. But some feeling nevertheless arose, and it was only enough to muffle the anger towards this sleeping woman.

It was a frosty day in this harsh snowy winter. There was no one in the house. Bagila agreed with her fellow students to go to the library, there was still an hour and a half left before the appointed time. Loneliness, as you know, can lead human thought to the most unexpected turns, especially in a spacious, five-room apartment, crammed with beautiful, upholstered furniture and books that no one will ever read...

She knew that Jasyn had returned long ago, but she could find a reason to talk to him. Several times Bagila went to the pay phone, tried to dial a number. But, having wound up three or four numbers, she began to breathe heavily, her face lit up with dry fire, and she jumped out of the booth. Staying alone in the house, she approached the home phone several times, standing on the bedside table in the corridor. But every time she is overcome by prickling shame. Dialling six numbers was beyond her strength. It seemed vicious enough to her already that she was approaching the telephone.

And now, after much worry and conflicting thoughts, she went to the phone. She slowly raised the phone to her ear. A monotone low buzzing. The device worked flawlessly. She was ready to convey her voice to Jasyn in a matter of seconds.

She dialled the first three digits calmly. On the fourth her hand trembled. She barely twisted the fifth digit, as if her finger had become a straw and was about to break off. There was one more left, the last one... She raised her index finger to the figure eight, the disk slowly spun... There was nothing to breathe. She closed her eyes as she heard long, intermittent beeps on the phone. One second, two seconds...

Then something cracked dryly, and then a cold, indifferent male voice rang out:

"Hello..."

Bagila couldn't open her mouth.

"Hello!" the man repeated irritably.

"Jasyn!" She gasped

"Hello, what is it?!"

"Hello!" Bagila blurted out, afraid that now he would hang up, and she would not have enough strength to call a second time.

"Hey... What do you need?"

"When did you arrive?"

"A while back. Who is it?"

"Have you... forgotten me? I'm..."

"What are you mumbling for! Who is speaking?"

"It's... Bagila..."

"Ah, I remember... I wanted to call you, but there was always no time. Do you have business with me?"

Bagila hung up. "Do you have business with me?" Those words, like a jet of water, nearly knocked her off her feet. Her soul, for the umpteenth time, through his fault, fell, shattered to smithereens.

She threw herself face down on the bed. "Do you have business with me? How rude! Jerk! Why did I call him, why? I'm so stupid! That's what I deserve. You are the one to blame! You wanted to hear his voice? There, you got it!"

She was awakened by the loud slamming of the front door in the corridor. Bagila recognised Sargel by the sound of his footsteps. She quickly moved to a chair and grabbed a book. The phone rang. Sargel picked up the phone. Bagila, remembering her skirmish with Mancia, tiptoed to the door and closed it.

Sargel's footsteps were heard. He walked straight to her room. Slightly delayed at the entrance. The door opened cautiously. Bagila felt Sargel's sharp gaze on her back. Why is he looking at her like that?

"Bagila!" It was clear that he was about to call out to her, but she shuddered all the same. Trying not to look at his face, she half turned around.

"Someone asking for you... At the phone," he said pointedly. Bagila shrugged her shoulders in surprise and walked past Sargel to the device. She could tell from his irritated voice and raised chin that Sargel didn't like the caller at all.

"Hello," she said in a startlingly indifferent voice.

"It's me. Are you offended again?"

"Jasyn! It's him! God! What do I say to him?!" The thought raced through her head.

"Do you hear me?" Asked a voice that was velvety and at the same time heavy as lead. "I'm asking, do you hear me?"

"Yes... What do you want?"

"Who answered the phone?"

"Are you calling to find out about this?"

"Sounds like a very nasty guy."

"I'm not going to discuss my relatives with you."

"It seems like every other person can be angry like you, it surprises me. Do you have free time tomorrow?"

"No."

"Find some, please." He chuckled softly. "I never begged anyone before. Weird..."

"I have no time. Good luck!"

"Just don't hang up the phone, they only do that in bad movies. So, tomorrow at exactly six in the evening at the Almaty hotel. Don't be late. Come. And then you can hate me for the rest of your life. Although you can hate me every second prior. Anyway, forgot to say hello!"

Bagila remained standing, holding the handset in her hand. "How confident! What a jerk! He thinks I'll run! But no, that's not happing!" She thought.

Realising that the conversation was over, Sargel left the office.

"Bagila," he addressed in such an official tone, as if speaking at the court. "Maybe you will be offended, but I will say this... Do not talk to this person anymore. He has no culture, no respect for people! He gets on a call with strangers, hears a man's voice in the receiver and does not even say hello. 'You want me to call Bagila?' And that's all. And his voice, what a horrible voice! So rude! You know what I mean?"

"Yes, I do!" Bagila, like a child, nodded her head and, not being able to process all of the information, went to her room. Closing the door behind her, she remembered what Jasyn and Sargel had said about each other and smiled involuntarily. But the reason for this smile was still mainly Jasyn's call. He called her, and that is the most important thing in her life!

The next day, at exactly six in the evening, Bagila stood in front of the Almaty hotel. After a long and heated discussion with Malika, it was decided that they should go on a date. The woman could not allow this story to continue. Oh, and it was him that invited her…! The fact that he is married, he has children, Malika did not care. She was much more interested in the fact that Jasyn was inviting Bagila to the hotel. But, after thinking this way and that, they considered it a mere accident.

During the discussion, they even burst into tears, admitting with tears that the life of a woman consists only of defeats, forgiveness and concessions.

The fact that Bagila went on this date was the very first major retreat in her life and it was completely natural for Malika, who simply could not imagine how you can pout when Madiev himself calls you!

Having approached the entrance of the hotel, Bagila hesitated, not knowing what to do next, and then Jasyn appeared from around the corner, as if following her from the side (perhaps this was the case.)

Eighteen years... This is quite enough time for a person to see the most diverse relationships between people, to be surprised, to despair, to hate and even to deteriorate. Bagila, meanwhile, looked with naive curiosity at this world, seeing only purity, the sun and a reason for sensual experiences. Of course, she had already dated guys more than once before and even kissed... But her meeting with Jasyn was her first real date, and her little heart had not found peace since yesterday, fluttering like a leaf in the wind. When Jasyn said hello, she barely answered him, she was out of breath. And only at that moment did Bagila have time to look at him and immediately quickly lowered her eyes. Not a trace of yesterday's pride was left, she now looked like a kid, trusting him to the point of stupidity.

"Ah, she really likes me," thought Jasyn. "Looks like she fell in love!"

He always stayed away from words such as "love", "feeling" and "fidelity." In any case, he had not yet met people in his life who would prove to him the reality of these words, moreover, by nature he was prone to tough relationships, and these words pricked him like bristles. And he also hated people who used them often. He never read love poems, he noted with displeasure on Tolstoy's statements about love, about feelings, at the end of Dostoevsky's sentimental novel "White Nights" he nervously wrote: "Does he really believe in ideal people?!" For every occasion in life, he had clear judgments. In particular, he firmly held to the opinion that romance and true love are an illusion, they confuse a person, interfere with an accurate understanding of life! He persistently cultivated this life psychology in his work. "His characters are not human. They are superhuman, devoid of human feelings," someone once criticised him. Others agreed, arguing that it was high time to look life straight in the eye. How long will humanity pay attention to the weaknesses of its individuals. Jasyn's works are a new realistic view of today's prose on life, his allies would say, and only predators and sentimental fools are afraid of this view. Jasyn, who is never lost for words, lingered a little and lost the words prepared for the meeting.

"Let's go," he said somewhat embarrassedly, pointing at the car waiting for them, he wasn't sure if she would follow him.

Bagila did not resist, did not even ask where he wanted to take her. She followed him as if spellbound. Jasyn put her in the front seat, and he sat in the back. It was not in his mind to sit down like that, but it was as if someone had ordered him to stay away from the girl. "Peculiar!" he said to himself, closing the door behind her. "Is this really happening to me?! No, it's impossible!"

They drove carefully along the icy avenue, he felt that he was still cramped. What was it? Is he really that lost in front of Bagila?! In addition, his speech, usually knocked down, harsh, collapsed like an old fence, and, most amazingly, for the first time in his life, his chest warmed when he looked at Bagila.

In the thirty-one years of his life, of course, he knew women, and quite a few. Among them there were all sorts: seasoned and joyful, beautiful and not so much... But his heart had never beaten faster than usual. Every time it was the same thing - he subordinated the woman to himself, exercised over her the power of his desire, and that was all. He saw only what was before his eyes, nothing more.

He wrote about it in a more complicated, more interesting way and the women were often offended by Jasyn, accusing him of god knows what. They loved him so much that as soon as he asked them to stop, they gave up... His sharp, thoughtful eyes, iron logic, bold reasoning stood out like a sore thumb, wherever he was: among historians, economists, linguists, archaeologists, artists and actors – the eyes of all the women around would rest on him.

Many women demanded confessions of high love and thus caused bouts of irritable arguments. He believed that there are two qualities in a person that are born and die of their own free will, these are love and hatred, and to justify an ordinary connection with lofty words is the most primitive meanness.

They came to the theatre and watched the tragedy of a foreign playwright. But it did not arouse any interest in Bagila. Since the start of her studies in Almaty, this was her third time going to the theatre, but for some reason she paid attention only to the acting. They talked about this during the intermission.

After the performance, Jasyn got a taxi. Bagila sat in front, he sat behind again. And once more, she didn't ask where they were going.

It snowed heavily yesterday, and it was difficult to drive. The car wobbled every now and then, for a long time its treads screeched on the ice at the intersections, unable to pick up speed. When they finally got out onto the straight avenue, Jasyn suddenly, without hiding his surprise, said:

"This is the first time I've met a girl like you."

Bagila turned to him.

"How come?"

"After all, a person in this situation would ask where it is they are being taken!"

"I already know. Why ask?"

Jasyn, stunned, was silent. Only after a while he asked apprehensively:

"How do you know?"

"Your phone number starts with 39..."

"So what?!"

"And we're just approaching the area where phone numbers start like that."

"With such observation-," said the amazed Jasyn, "-you should have entered the law faculty! Though to be fair, I don't really like it either, you have to really look after yourself in both!"

"Why is it like that?! You say, specialising as a historian is not for me, making observation does not suit me, even my name doesn't suit you, how can I live on?" She turned to him and smiled, raising her eyebrows questioningly.

"How can you live on…? As a standard of beauty, you can be taken under the protection of UNESCO and put in some cold museum."

"What will I do when I'm old?"

"Then you will stand as a model of aged beauty. But to be in clothes or not, this will be decided by the international commission."

Bagila quickly forced the smile off her face and looked away.

"Thanks for that, at least," she said, not concealing her resentment.

This instantly flashing half-childish resentment, and eager pride, and the way she sat down, raising her chin, made Jasyn laugh, but he could not help but notice that at that moment she became even more beautiful. Having reached Jasyn's house, they got out of the car.

Bagila did not really think about where and why he was taking her, but, having entered the entrance and stepped onto the stairs, she felt a tremor in her legs. "He's a stranger, after all," she thought, "well, of course, a complete stranger. And I followed him here like his tail. This is how you humiliate yourself. Who is at his house?

What if his wife is here? How will I introduce myself? What will he call me? In a completely foreign house, in the middle of the night!"

"I… I should probably leave," she said, stopping resolutely on the landing on the second floor. "Yes, I'm not staying. Sorry…"

Jasyn looked at her, somehow suddenly embarrassed.

"I beg you, I can forgive everything," he said. "If you leave now, it will be a mockery of your trust in me and my pure attitude towards you."

"Perhaps," she whispered, moving her lips a little. "Where are we going?"

"To the fourth floor."

"Let's go then…"

There was no one in Jasyn's house except his father. The wife, having taken time off from work for a week, left with her children to go to a village for the winter holidays. His father, who was quite sick and old, was lying in the back room. Opening the door with his key, Jasyn pointed to the hanger, as if saying "hang your stuff up here," and then went to his father.

"Well, father, how are you?" she heard.

"Thank you, son, not bad," the father answered.

"Is there a letter from Sophia Loren?"

"God damn it, no."

Bagila hung her sheepskin coat on a hanger, took off her boots and froze, not knowing what to do next. "Why don't you go?" she heard again.

"I'll go if you give me travel allowances."

Jasyn, laughing loudly, waved his hand to Bagila towards the right room. Bagila obediently went where she was directed.

"There's a sly one!" Now Jasyn's voice was heard more muffled. "It turns out that I have to pay travel expenses to your love?"

"That's the only way," said the father, coughing.

"Well then lie down. Perhaps Sophia Loren will come with Ma. Will you drink tea?"

"No. Later."

"What about coffee?"

"Why the hell would I want it. Do you want me to hoot like an owl all night?"

Jasyn laughed out loud again and went to Bagila, saying casually: "All right, if you need me, just call." Bagila, marvelling at such an unusual manner of communication between father and son, heard Jasyn in the hall taking off his outer clothing and boots. She looked around carefully, saw three shelves lined with books, and felt dizzy. She felt like a small helpless creature. "It's a mockery of oneself. Is it possible to read so much?" she thought, experiencing wounded pride, since the owner of these books knew much more than she did. As soon as she had time to put her thoughts in order, Jasyn entered the room. As soon as he crossed the threshold, he switched on the bright ceiling light and the floor lamp, he reached the desk on the other side of the room, leaning on it and turning to face Bagila.

"Forgive me," he said, looking at Bagila with a soft smile.

"I see how it is. And I thought he was your son-in-law," Bagila joked, referring to their manner of speaking.

"I have been talking with him like that for a long time... I am the first-born of that horseman. After all, as long as the grandfather is alive, the first child does not belong to the father. I was raised by my grandfather. Grew up in his arms. And after me, my father had two more girls who quickly jumped out to get married, and after them, Sophia Loren didn't give birth anymore. After the death of my grandfather, my father began to court me and eventually pulled me over to him. So, we play pranks on each other, like peers."

"Who is Sophia Loren?"

"What do you mean who?! She's a famous film actress. But to us – it's nickname for the old woman that's married to my horseman dad." He laughed. "She, along with my wife and children, went to the village. That old woman is absolutely convinced that her grandchildren cannot move around the earth without her."

"Why do you call her that?"

"Ha, we don't call her that just because! A long time ago, the real Sophia Loren came to Moscow when they were screening the movie 'Sunflowers'. Then my father went to Moscow with me. We, along with several Kazakh writers, met the actress in the hotel we were staying at. My dad saw her too. When we came to our room, I asked my father: "Well, did you like her?" He waved his hand: "Are you overeating donkey brains?! She's no better than my old woman. If you dress her properly, then Saparkul will easily surpass Sophie." I asked, "Well, why don't a pay the bride a price and marry you to her? My dad flatly refused, too skinny, he said. Since then, we've been calling my mother that anytime we're talking to him, just like you heard."

Bagila laughed, a silvery chuckle.

"Interesting! No one in our family would even dream of saying that. Everything is in its place. The father is the father, the mother is the mother, the child is the child. And compared to everyone I know, moreover then not, the place of each family member is marked too clearly."

"It is not necessary for such a hierarchy to exist in every family." Jasyn lit a cigarette. "How about dinner?"

"No need."

"I don't want it either. Let's kill time. I really regret to lose those minutes that could of satisfied the stomach. We'd better drink coffee."

Jasyn went to the kitchen. Immediately there was the rumbling of a tap, the lid of the coffee maker rang, a lit match hissed. Then the doors of the refrigerator and cabinets slammed shut.

Jasyn, smiling slightly, returned to the room.

"You know…" he began to speak from the doorway and fell silent only to settle down in an armchair across from Bagila. "A person spends half of his life eating and sleeping. Sometimes it seems to me that people are only created to eat their fill, sleep their fill and die. Sitting down at the table three times a day is almost crazy, but there are those who eat from morning to night. In my opinion, the almighty is a big egoist, he only thinks about himself. If you read the Bible and the Koran, then you might think that both God and Allah created man solely out of condescension. Is that so? God created man for his own pleasure. Tired of idleness, he invented man out of boredom, and, as if not finding a more normal planet in the universe, he settled us away from other worlds on a planet called Earth. People, like busy ants, began a collective existence. And although they were given a limited time to live, although they buried each other by the thousands, their existence seemed to them eternal, like that of the almighty. They surrendered and are surrendered to the meaningless everyday life. This is beneficial to the creator. Looking at our lives, he dies of laughter, he always has a merry spectacle. If not for us, he would have dried up from boredom long ago. Still, the creator's fantasy worked well. Well done to him!"

Jasyn smiled bitterly. Bagila did not understand who he was laughing at, at God? At humans or at himself? Suddenly, she became afraid. She had never seen a man who would say nasty things about god. And now there was one sitting opposite her, smoking a cigarette with might and main, and blasphemed not only humans, but also the creator. She didn't read either the Bible or the Koran, she didn't think about god at all, but still she was creeped out... Okay, maybe that's just Jasyn, what about his father?! Like his son, and he also joked about Allah in a conversation with his son. She met with Jasyn only for the second time. During this time, she managed to hate him several times, forget this hatred and yearn several times... From any word that Jasyn said, even from his mechanical glance, she lost her head, as if from a sip of champagne, and immediately realised how petty and notorious she was. If they meet, how many more times will she have to boil, cool down, cry and laugh? Bagila subconsciously felt that it would be more than once or twice.

"Okay, let's stop this conversation," said Jasyn, pressing the cigarette butt into the ashtray. "How long can you be with me?"

"Zero minutes," she said, dispersing the thick to-bacco smoke with her hand. "Because I should be home by now. Moreover, I allowed the time allotted to me to overrun by two hours."

"Oh, thanks!" Jasyn said embarrassingly, opening the window. "Not for the frankness, but for the resource-fulness."

"Do you like to speak beautifully?"

"No, no so much. But I'm not against beautiful

turns. Words, you know, determine the biggest events in the world: from peace to war... Excuse me, it seems that the coffee has boiled?"

Jasyn moved hastily to the kitchen. He brought coffee on a tray according to all the rules of serving and put it on a low table that stood between their chairs.

"I understand," he poured the coffee into cups, "you were brought up in a completely different environment. Everything that I say and do, even the fact that I brought you to my house, may seem rude, unnatural to you. But I'm not going to fit in with everyone. Any person cannot be satisfied with absolutely everything, even the almighty is far from always being satisfied. Is that not the case? But let's leave god alone for a moment. The most important thing is to correctly understand the meaning of your deeds and words. Everything else is secondary in priority, so to speak, the technical side of existence..."

"Yes, you say and do a lot differently than everyone else," said Bagila, taking a sip of coffee. "Don't be offended by this but... Do you love your wife?"

Jasyn chuckled but didn't answer. He looked straight at Bagila. Again, she could not stand the sharp, cold look and, as if afraid of burning her eyes, instantly lowered her eyelashes and began to fuss.

Bagila's cheeks blushed, biting her lips, she began to twist the cup in front of her with thin long fingers. "Why did I even come here? Indeed, why?" She asked herself, not knowing where to hide from the awkwardness "Why do I feel so uncomfortable? Maybe I really was raised wrong?" She was ready to burst into tears. "If it turns out that I'm wrong - that means I'm not like him?! But does everyone have to be like Jasyn? Of course not, that's stupid! I should tell him all this and leave this house. Now, immediately!"

"Okay, okay, I'll answer you," Jasyn suddenly said, completely startling Bagila. "You most likely wanted to ask something different, something like: why did I invite you here…? I didn't have any ulterior motive and still don't. I just wanted to talk to you in this setting. I don't know why, but maybe I do… Understand me correctly, you are like a degenerate falcon, and it hurts me that you, along with the ravens and owls, are flying around in the same grey flock as everyone else. In order for a person to become a person, only a natural gift is not enough for them, everything depends on the environment in which they are located. Remember this, otherwise I wouldn't be talking to you. How about some more coffee?"

"How many years is your father older than you?" Bagila asked harshly.

From an unexpected question, Jasyn straightened up in his chair.

"Exactly as much as he is older."

"You seem to have confused adults with children. You talk to your father like a small child, but to me like an old woman."

Jasyn froze, staring at her. His cold eyes warmed up,

he enjoyed what Bagila said, and did not hide it.

They fell silent. Jasyn was not going to answer the question. For no apparent reason, he suddenly began to think that life passes like a summer downpour, and that the great 'time' quietly steals life from everyone from the moment of their birth. When they are barely conceived, these creatures begin to age.

For the first time, he felt that one of the main thefts of time was tenderness and love for a woman. No, he is still strong and can take over the heart of anyone, and hers too... Let five, ten years pass, he still will not grow old, if necessary, he will live without paying attention to women, without love for them. Jasyn's soul was disturbed by an unexpected discovery: in the thirty-one years of his life, it turns out that he had lost one of the main qualities of a person - to love carelessly, without worrying about anything...

From this thought, Jasyn felt anguish, he began to lose what is irreplaceable... But then another thought flashed: "You still have a lot to lose, so don't despair."

Rising, he went to the window and parted the curtains.

"Look, it's snowing," Jasyn said quietly with a sort of bilious bitterness.

Bagila approached him. As on that autumn day, when they walked side by side from the cafe, this time she was strictly making sure, that god forbid, she does not touch Jasyn.

"Yes, snow… It's falling in flakes."

Jasyn looked at the snowfall, smiling imperceptibly at Bagila.

"Be a little quite will you. I have a feeling that you have completely exhausted me," he said.

"Again, with this…" Bagila said offendedly, not understanding how she could be exhausting him.

Jasyn stood with his hands in his pockets and spoke as if he hadn't heard her threats.

"And in the world, it is snowing quietly, carelessly," he said as if to himself. "Everyone is busy with their own lives. Nobody cares about each other. See that eight-story building over there? How many people, how many destinies are in it… Everyone who lives there, has someone they love, someone they hate. Some are scurrying about in the kitchen, others are withered in front of the TV, others are in the bedroom… Look, what an interesting picture: there is a young woman in swimming trunks and a bra opening the curtains, but they should have been closed…"

Bagila looked at the woman and lowered her head.

"And tomorrow they will all scatter around like ants from a fire. In the evening, they'll go home… They will cook dinner, eat it and go to bed. And rightly so, you need to take a break, because tomorrow you will run again. Each of them has children, big and small. Everyone strives to achieve something, fights with someone, suffers defeat from someone. And here, you see, the snow is falling as if nothing had happened. It seems to be stupid, but at such moments I feel especially keenly how small we are and how great nature is. Whether you die or are born, it snows no matter what... What do you think of that?" He half turned to Bagila.

"You ordered me to be quiet, and I am silent. You won't hear another word from me."

"Ah! Again, you pout like a little child! Damn it, was it really impossible to notice the importance of the moment! However, it's good that you didn't notice. Well, are you going home?"

"Yes. And immediately."

"I'll walk you out. They're probably missing you at home and are going scold you for what the world is worth."

He helped put on her sheepskin coat, gave her boots. And when she came to the door, he realised that while she was there, he felt better than ever, and now, as soon as she leaves, the emptiness and bile that have been eating him up lately are rising up again.

He took her in a taxi to her house. He shook her hand in farewell. When she shook his hand, he suddenly leaned over and kissed her fingers, hot and dry. Bagila carefully released her hand and slowly slipped on the glove, blushing crimson with shame. It was unbearable for both of them to be silent, and Jasyn said:

"You know what, I still don't like your name."

"Is that what bothers you the most?"

"That's it... Nothing worries me as much as that." Jasyn somehow grinned pathetically. "Well, all the best. God bless, see you later."

He walked sideways to the car, sat down, slammed the door, and the taxi rolled down the dark street, splattering wet, dirty snow with its tires.

The next year, in the summer, Sargel finally defended his dissertation. Having achieved the coveted title of Doctor of Science, he calmed down and threw a banquet. Everyone who took part in calming him down was invited, some leaders of higher education, the entire department, and close relatives came. A special invitation was sent to Karatai by courier (Sargel liked this idea very much: to send a person with his letter to Karate, and he did not stint, giving one of his young relatives "travel allowances" in both directions). Besides that, Sargel called Karatai twice, asking with exaggerated solicitude if anything would harm his arrival.

Karatai never learned to refuse those who were unpleasant to him, especially relatives, and although he had enough work, which could serve as a worthy reason not to go, he went to Sargel's banquet anyway. Since Karatai appeared in Almaty, his friend from the Ministry of Higher Education ended up behind Sargel's table for the second time, which made him delighted to the point of madness. But, given his position and the delicacy of the situation, (Sargel, Karatai and he knew the "history" of the doctoral's attainment very well) he asked through Karatai to gather a narrow circle with his participation. Sargel, seeing that his fellow workers continued to discuss his brilliant attainment in astonishment, breathed a sigh of relief when his benefactor asked for privacy.

Last year, after a warm conversation with the rector, who did not forget his promise to talk with Sargel in more detail after returning from abroad, Sargel, taking advantage of the arrival of Karatai, invited him to a meeting with the rector and a person from the ministry - all with their wives – who came to visit, and everything was decided in his house. Sargel was very pleased with the weight of Karatai behind this venerable table, his mind, and his wise words. This meant that Karatai's participation would lead to sure luck. True, after that evening, Sargel still had one caustic feeling, which then sharpened him for a long time. Twice he noticed how the rector, who was a dozen years younger, exchanged glances with Malika several times, joked with her, and that damned wife answered him with a smile.

Now by inviting the rector to the banquet, Sargel suffered a lot, but decided that his favour was much more valuable than Malika's smiles... Having compiled the list of guests, Sargel deliberately did not enter the rector's name on it and let Malika to look through the list. Malika realised in no time that Sargel could not just forget the rector, it was tantamount to the end of the world, and that this "forgetfulness" hides petty deceit.

She carefully studied the list for a long time and demonstratively returned it to Sargel, saying: "That's right, you haven't forgotten anyone." Sargel became suspicious again: "She said that on purpose. So, she has something to hide from me. That cursed womaniser, he's no leader!"

"How could you forget!" he exclaimed, not taking his eyes off his wife. "And what about the rector? I can't believe you!

"Oh god!" Malika rolled her eyes. Then she shook her head and decided to settle accounts with Sargel for his petty cunning. "He's a fine man! Soft, playful! It is imperative we call him, he'll come with an adorned company."

An electrical shiver ran through Sargel's hide.

"Well, since you're asking like that, you should call him," he said significantly, filling every word with fog. He wrote the rector's name in block letters and put a dot in such a way that the paper under the pen burst. Then he threw the pen on the table, lifted his chin, sticking out his throbbing Adam's apple, and putting his hands behind his back whilst leaving the house.

At the banquet they sat like two enemies, watching each other with unblinking eyes dry with hatred.

At the general banquet held at the table sat Karatai, who in two days of fuss in Sargel's house, managed to resolve all the necessary issues in the city. After paying homage at Sargel's house, he took Sargel, Malika, and his daughter to the mountains. He wanted to be with his eldest, and at the same time Karatai decided to see how and in what direction her life had gone during her stay in the big city.

They had a light lunch in an open restaurant, once again celebrating Sargel's doctorate.

July was blazing in the mountains. It was impossible to sit in one place for a long time, and they decided to climb a slope overgrown with fir trees.

"How nice!" exclaimed Karatai as he reached a turbulent stream that eroded a rocky slope, he sat down on a warm stone.

"At least for the sake of this you should come to Almaty more often," Bagila said jokingly, grabbing her father by the neck.

"If only I knew about this stream!" Karatai laughed, and everyone followed him, laughing sincerely and nonchalantly.

Sargel also laughed, as Malika would put it, completely in sync with Karatai.

"Dad! Why are you making a girl out of me!" Bagila pouted capriciously. "I'm not a child after all!"

"Well, do we really have to speak officially!" Karatai kissed his daughter on the cheek.

"Yes, let's talk officially! Every Soviet person has the right to work and rest. And you do not obey these constitutional rules. How can you violate the Constitution and rule the whole area! If you work with people, you should find time for this position of nature, however, they do not talk about it at regional assets and the connection between the murmur of the stream and the increase in the number of sheep has not yet been established. All that so you can work without rest…" Bagila burst out laughing and rushed to kiss her father. "Well, give up, daddy?

"That's it, daughter, you've got me by the tail."

"Sur," interrupted Malika. "Leave your father alone, let him rest, really. And then I'll be offended if you, Karatai, forgot that I'm here!"

"It's okay," Sargel hurried, shaking small stones out of his boot. "Let her talk to her father."

"What did you say?! What does it mean – 'Sur', 'Sar'?" Karatai asked, raising his eyebrows.

"Sur means painting, and Sar means Sargel." Malika quickly kicked off her sandals and dipped her feet into the icy water.

Karatai chuckled and laughed heartily.

"Well, Malika, your imagination is boundless! Maybe you can think of something like that for me too?" He wiped his tears from laughter and looked with pleasure at Malika's feet, white in the mountain water.

Malika instantly caught this look, raised her legs from the stream, waited for the water to drain, and reached for her sandals, forgetting about her short dress… That was a strong blow! Sargel swallowed the mountain air like pieces of ice: he simply could not watch Karatai laugh.

Then Bagila came up with the idea of picking strawberries in the thicket. Here they dispersed, and she was left alone with her father.

"Dad, remember last year, when we were travelling here, you kicked a guy out of the train compartment?"

Karatai, carried away by the search for berries, unbent, thought and shook his head negatively.

"Well, how could you forget! Such a thin guy, with long hair... We were traveling in a two-seater compartment. Remember?"

"Ah! Yes, I remember something like that. Indeed, I cast out some idiot."

"You didn't cast him out but kicked him out like a puppy." Karatai carefully looked at his daughter:

"And what?! Why are you talking about it?"

"Because that jerk is a famous writer. His name is Jasyn Madiev. Did you know that?"

Karatai threw the berries under his feet, took out a handkerchief and thoroughly dried his hands.

"The first time I've heard of him. Madiev? No, I don't know him... So, what about it?"

"Nothing special. I just wanted to tell you that that young man turned out to be the most popular writer today."

"What a disaster!" Karatai smiled benevolently. "Is he really the most popular?"

"Daddy, don't you feel sorry that everything turned out like it did?" Bagila, trying to hide her mood, kissed her father coquettishly.

"What's there to be sorry about?" Karatai asked, changing to the tone he used to speak with Jasyn. "I don't know him, and I don't want to know him."

"But you don't know any of writers…"

"Bagila!" Karatai stopped his daughter with a shout. "You studied in Almaty for only a year and, apparently, decided that you could argue with me?! I have other knowledge and a different position. A real father always brings up a child in such a way that they respect what's being said! So stop with this nonsense!"

Bagila bit her tongue. She didn't want to talk to her father about that guy anymore. Such an angry reaction from her father fell like a shadow on her soul, Karatai quickly understood this and stroked his daughter on the head.

"Don't be angry with me," he said so that Bagila wanted to cuddle up to her father and cry. "There are too many people in this world who are angry with me. Don't be one of them."

Bagila sighed convulsively, a barely perceptible chill to her father remained. She knew: her father would never be different; it was too late for him to change. Until the end of his days, he will be so tough, self-confident - even when he is completely wrong. Thinking about it, she felt sorry for him.

In the evening, Karatai presented Sargel with a thousand rubles in honour of the attainment, had a quick dinner and flew home.

PART TWO

On New Year's Eve, Sargel received his Ph.D. He was convinced that after defending his dissertation, all the scientists of Almaty stopped their work and were only concerned with ensuring that the attestation commission did not approve his doctoral thesis at all costs. Sargel informed Karatai about all the insidiousness of his colleagues both in letters and by phone. At the last conversation, Karatai broke loose and, unexpectedly even for himself, shouted at his brother. Sargel drooped for several days, as if struck by a knife. He muttered that the end of the world had come, and his affairs were rubbish. All night, not knowing sleep, he paced along the worn old parquet between the kitchen and the corridor. Listening to the creaking of the floorboards under her husband's feet, Malika noted: "Kitchen, kitchen - corridor." These home walks of Sargel led him to a wild decision. He made a dash for Moscow. But apparently, there was no one in the attestation commission who would have met him with an enthusiastic exclamation "O dear Sir Sargel!" Sargel returned home emaciated, with deeply sunken eyes. On ordinary days, he looked at people with distrust, walked, taking on a dead weight of jealousy and bile, and after this incident he completely lost his peace. "You don't pity me, it doesn't matter to you," he repeated whiningly at home. "They don't want me to become a doctor because they envy me. They all enter my house with curiosity and leave with envy. All of them are enemies, everyone! In our time, there can be no friends, everyone wants to snatch things for themselves, only for themselves! I don't trust anyone. How can I trust others if my own thoughts are against me?! My wife, that's right? A man's first enemy is his wife!"

Malika knew well that a man can speak out of malice, sinking lower than a woman. And if you show restraint, wait a little while, the reckless anger recedes, he will again become a man. But the external state of Sargel was not like a mountain river, as if throwing stones; his character from birth was not bubbling, but quietly, stinkingly spiteful, falling asleep all around with the ashes of mute hatred. She stopped arguing with her husband, went to work early in the morning and, under any pretext, returned late. Sargel, as before, met her with an incredulous look, humiliating questions, demanded, frowning his eyebrows: "Stop, please!" And suddenly he received a rebuff, which plunged Sargel into confusion. He saw with fear that Malika would stop at nothing if he brought her to a white heat.

These dreary unpleasant days were left behind, they were preparing for the New Year holiday with special enthusiasm.

"Malika," Sargel said to his wife when they had established a good relationship and he was lying next to her. "This New Year is special! We'll meet it at the doctor's house. Remember that!"

"Ah, damn it!" Maliki said to herself. "Look at that, what a braggart! We know very well how you became a doctor. Rewrote the history of three districts in ten years – it's all you. Who else needs it? What is this writing for? You went only twice to the districts and was afraid to leave the house, always jealous of me. And that's supposed to be science!"

"Of course, we will meet it properly," Malika agreed indifferently, tired of arguing with her husband.

Returning from work in the evening, Malika saw that Sargel was pale, with the look of a lonely poor fellow, he was sitting on the sofa in front of the wide-open doors. Malika immediately realised that no matter how picky Sargel got, before the holiday, especially before the "doctor's New Year," he would not turn pale because of some trifle. So, she expected a big fight. She deliberately undressed for a long time, trying to guess what awaits her and what she needs to be ready for. Putting on light slippers, she moved to the kitchen, doing her best to ignore Sargel, but as soon as she crossed the threshold, she was stopped by a sharp cry:

"Malika!"

Turning around, she looked at her husband in exaggerated surprise.

"Don't be in a such hurry, I've had enough of that morning salad," Sargel said, suddenly switching to a more formal tone. "That salad is the epitome of a culinary blunder, it was prepared quickly, thoughtlessly and completely tastelessly. This only confirms my suspicions. Much to my regret!" Sargel stood up with solemn sorrow. "Sit down here," he pointed to the sofa from which he had just risen.

"Sar, for god's sake, tell it like it is, or I'll get up and leave," Malika could not stand it, fussing on the edge of the sofa...

"I lost my appetite because of you, but not for this reason, do you think that before such a special holiday, I wanted to have this conversation? Of course not! The point today is..."

"For god's sake, keep it short. You're not in a meeting!" Sargel did not listen to Malika. He steadily continued his speech.

"What I discovered does not fit in with virtue and honesty in the relationships of people, especially spouses, whose unity is determined by mutual honesty and dependence..."

"So?" She felt like she was going crazy.

"So, dear Malika," he lifted his chin, clearing his

throat, "I finally found irrefutable proof of my suspicions."

Malika's heart skipped a beat, but she, without showing any sign, raised careless eyes to her husband.

"This cigarette butt is the proof!" Sargel said, opening his palm, showed Malika a Medeo cigarette butt. "I remember well the last time you smoked in this house, it was a long time ago, but this cigarette butt was completely fresh. So, you smoked it in the house when I was in Moscow. But was it really necessary to throw the cigarette butt under the sofa?! What a lack of respect, what stupidity!"

Malika sighed in exasperation. Well, that's exactly what she was afraid of. While Sargel dangled at the capital, she, Bagila and Jasyn went out to a restaurant in Koktyube. It was there that Malika met Madiev. She took a liking to him immediately.

He immediately fascinated Malika with his concepts, his pure assessments of people, his mind-blowing education, she had never even heard of such a person before! Well, it's necessary to have your own opinion on any issue, to speak so freely, easily, raising yourself above the vanity of life. Yes, she was infinitely far from him! "Why aren't all people like him?" she thought then. "Why? Well, maybe not all, but at least half, maybe one quarter of people could be like Jasyn. Why are they too lazy to rise a little higher above themselves, why do they love a grey monotonous life?" She mentally compared the best men she knew with Jasyn and laughed involuntarily.

As soon as they left the restaurant, Malika really wanted to express her affection for Jasyn, to somehow prolong such a wonderful evening, and she invited him into the house.

Everything was wonderful! However, one thing was not good: after Jasyn's departure, she felt completely illiterate.

Malika became bitter. She understood well that between them lay a gigantic abyss that she could never overcome. But no matter what happened, she would not hesitate to rush to him, but as soon as Malika began to think about it, Bagila appeared before her.

That evening, while cleaning up after a guest, Malika accidentally spilled the ashtray.

Then, shutting her bedroom door tightly behind her, she wept for a long time in bed because she had never yet had the good fortune to live at least a minute as she liked, because she was now forever deprived of the right to choose where her life should go. She was crying, angry that women's happiness is completely different from men's, that one take-off is not enough for a woman to become happy, and that a woman's happiness is so dependent on a man.

Now, seeing the cigarette butt in Sargel's palm, she shuddered, she remembered that hard night... For a normal person, something as stupid as a cigarette butt could not become a reason for a quarrel, and it's even a shame to talk about it. But to Sargel, oh, to him, there was a lot of meaning behind it! This means that there was a man in the house, a man during his absence! Which means that in the house, his house, there was a secret meeting between that man and his wife! She was left with two options: either admit any accusation or repeat "I don't know." Looking down at the cigarette butt in Sargel's palm, she shook her head, shrugged.

"I don't understand anything," Malika said, as if inviting her beloved Sargel to reveal the secret together.

"Oh yeah? And I understand everything!" Sargel clutched the priceless cigarette butt in his palm. "Now everything will be clear to you. Ertai, hey, Ertai! Well, come here!"

Understanding her husband's move, Malika, unable to restrain herself, jumped up from the sofa. "Bastard!" she thought furiously. "He got everything out of the kids! Damned old man!"

Seeing their parents' offended faces the children entered the living room, Malika realised that Sargel probably shouted, scared them with god knows what, maybe beat them to find out how everything was. Seeing their mother, the children involuntarily moved towards her, but Sargel stopped them.

"Ertai, repeat everything that you recently told me. Is it true that some uncle came to us?"

"It's true." The boy lowered his head.

"Tell me everything!"

"The uncle sat for a long time. And mum too. We were late for kindergarten the next day."

"Well done! Now go to your room!"

"Well, what objections do you have?" Sargel asked sarcastically, leaning towards his wife.

"None," Malika answered decisively, seeing that nothing could be corrected. "There is no other way out except for the recognition of the divorce."

Sargel listened with his head on his shoulder and his eyes wide.

"No, dear citizen, marriage is not your private affair alone," he shook his finger. "I will write a statement because the crime was committed by you. You, and not I, committed treason, you were the one who was morally wrong," he raised his voice "It was you, not me!"

"To hell with you. Write your statement. Write it right now. You know how to write; you are a doctor!" She sighed wearily and folded her face in her hands.

"At this age, it is certainly not easy for me to lose a wife for the second time," Sargel's voice suddenly trembled. "How will I face the public! What will be the fate of these two children! I can't stop thinking about it, I don't have a heart of stone. But there is also honour, conscience, and these circumstances are above all. In order for people to understand who is really to blame, I will write about everything openly. Of course, no one saw you in bed, but the appearance of a man in the house when the husband is away is…! Let's just say, I am in no hurry to find out what happened, we can find out in court!"

Malika saw more and more clearly that things were taking a sharp turn. She realised that if Sargel was not stopped, then a big drama would eventually arise due to a cigarette butt, Bagila would be disgraced, and Jasyn would lose his family.

"Sar," she pleaded. "I'm not afraid of anything. If I tell everything as it was, will you calm down then?"

"If you intend to repeat Bagila's little tale, then don't bother, it's a waste of time."

"Why? Is she home?!"

"Everyone is home. There were three women here in my absence, and all three are here now. But Mancia doesn't know anything, you didn't take her into your company. You needed intimacy!"

"Mancia is closer to me than to you, but you know her character, she avoids everyone."

"That's not what we're talking about," said Sargel, lifting his chin again. "So, who is this person? Speak!"

Sargel stopped looming around the room, resting his hands on the table, he hovered over his wife, tuning his ears to what she's about to say.

"A man shouldn't be doing this sort of thing… We'll just be harassing Bagila. Aren't you ashamed!"

"Interesting! It is not shameful to drag men into my house, but it is shameful to say who it was?! So, who was he? State his name, surname and position. Maybe I'll believe then that you're innocent."

"Is this a house or an intensive care unit where strangers cannot enter and where you cannot smoke?"

"Answer the question!"

"God, just understand! The one whose name and position you are so eager to know is the person Bagila liked. What's the use of asking about him? You're angry that we didn't tell you he was coming. And how should we have done to? To ring your doorbell in Moscow; to say that while you were gone, we did such and such and such and such?!"

"Don't hide behind Bagila. Depending on my relationship and trust with Karatai!"

From this idiotic thought, Malika ran out of patience. She fell silent, clutching her head, rage and anger, hatred boiled so violently in her chest that, more than anything in the world, she wanted to give up on everything, take the children and leave this house wherever her eyes look.

"You... you will kill me too," she said lastly. "You are a freak, not a man! Your cunning makes the dishonest seem like honest people. I said everything, decide the rest yourself, according to your conscience and honour." She stood up, staggering, as if the floor was shaking under her, and saw Bagila in the doorway with a tear-stained face swollen with tears.

"Lika," she said, ignoring Sargel. "Don't be upset. I'll go to a hostel. I understand that you find living here simply impossible."

Bagila really decided to leave Sargel's house, Malika realised this when she saw a suitcase and an attaché case at the girl's feet. Sargel had the look of a fool. Malika looked contemptuously at her husband, asking him with his eyes: "Well, did you achieve your goal?!"

With a purely feminine intelligence, she realised that, in truth, the departure of Bagila did not promise her any complications. Indeed, if she had not married Sargel, she would not have known Karatai, his many friends, his wife and children, and especially Bagila. In fact, they are complete strangers to each other. If anyone will feel bad, it will be their relative Sargel. She thought it over instantly, but she herself was afraid that she could think so badly. Malika also thought that kindness and love bring people together, and not family relations themselves, and that closeness through mutual kindness is stronger than family ties. During these one and a half years, she got so used to Bagila, became so close to her that she could not imagine life without her. She was deafened as if by thunder that a person close to her, to whom she entrusted her innermost, was going to leave. But Malika, restraining herself, waited for what Sargel would do.

"What is it? Do you want to tell me what's going on?" Sargel asked, clearly flustered.

"No, that's just the decision I made," said Bagila in a whisper. "Can I live the way I want? Isn't that right, Lika?" She looked at Malika, forcing a smile.

"Well, just like the devil, even if he laughs, even if he cries, you can't take your eyes off him!" Malika noted with envy.

Angry faces flashed before Sargel's eyes - Karatai, then his friends from the Ministry of Higher Education and the rector. If this doll voluntarily leaves his house, then powerful people will disappear for him like a dream. The fact that their disappearance or presence depended on the mean girl infuriated Sargel, but he began to speak calmly, even affectionately.

"We didn't do anything wrong to you," he began in the tone of a caring relative. "I have no right to teach you, but still, I will say this: sooner or later you will get married and start a family. And god forbid, if someone's lustful hand intervenes in your honest life, the snake of debauchery will crawl through your warm nest. You will probably behave even worse than me. Now, when I speak the pure truth, confirmed by physical evidence and children, one of you rears up like a wild horse, and the other demonstrates tribal pride. Do you think I should have silently finished smoking this cigarette butt? Is that what you want?! You are certainly guilty before me, but you will leave, what will people say, what will relatives in the village say?! What will Karatai think? Go put your things back!" He finally glared angrily at Malika, "Why are you standing there, help!"

Malika was glad that Sargel barked at her. She picked up Bagila's things, shouldered her towards her room. And then Mancia peeped out of the door opposite. She looked at them in such a way that it seemed, if by her will alone, they would be torn apart.

"How scary!" whispered Bagila, falling into her chair.

"What's scary?"

"Her glare! She always looks at me like that. What did I do to her?!"

"Who knows," Malika sighed somehow pitifully. "She can't stand me either. The poor girl does not even understand that she does not have a closer person than me, and who, if not me, should do her good. Whatever!" She frowned, making it clear that one could talk endlessly on this topic, but not now, when it was already dreary. "Tell me, why did you decide to leave me?"

"I knew that uncle Sargel would not let go of this," Bagila laughed.

Malika, rounding her eyes, piercingly looked at her.

"Oh, how clever you are! You knew he wouldn't let go?! Do you know how I will beat you for disrespecting Sargel like that?" She, having rolled the newspaper into a tube, began to hit Bagila on the back. "Take that! Take that!"

Having finished the "punishment", Malika hugged Bagila tightly, kissed her cheeks and forehead.

Bagila, freeing herself from the embrace, saw glittering tears in Malika's eyes. Again, Malika cried. From grief or joy? For the past or the present? Or for future…?

No one could answer this question, nor could Malika herself. She just got too worried in the last minutes, and suddenly she felt good, empty and cheerful, as if she had just begun to live.

A few days later, Karatai received a long, vague letter from Sargel with cryptic allusions. He had never received and never written such long and confusing messages. He immediately opened the letter, but could not read beyond the introduction, and then forgot about it, and the letter lay in his pocket for several days.

When Karatai finally read Sargel's letter, he felt unkind in his heart, although he did not understand the essence of his relative's reasoning.

Sargel hinted at a recent event in his house and asked that Karatai not tell anyone about this, even Bagila's mother, but, he says, he could not help but write about it, and that it was Karatai's duty as a father to know about this ordinary incident, and Sargel did not dare to remain silent... "I often think a lot about how our family should always be clean before society, before people, so that they don't slander us," Sargel ended the letter in this way.

Karatai, suppressing his annoyance, got to the bottom of Sargel's reasoning, sorting through words that looked like ant tracks. He read the letter at breakfast. Yesterday he was informed that the loss of livestock had begun at a remote state farm, and he was preparing to leave for the farm in the morning together with Turgat, who was the acting head of the agricultural department.

The manager retired, and Karatai insisted on the bureau of the district committee to entrust the department to Turgat. While his wife was putting breakfast on the table, he read the letter again.

After drinking hot tea with pastries, Karatai got up from the table.

"You'll spoil your stomach, eat like a human being," the wife grumbled, as usual, although she knew that Karatai never ate heavily in the morning.

"The car is waiting, I must go."

"What kind of letter do you have? The one you are reading so intently."

"I don't know... A complaint against you!"

"Who is it that doesn't like me?" she asked, supporting the joke.

"A student... She writes that you treat her like a girl."

"Bagila, right?"

"Would I really stay quiet? It's just Sargel with all his nonsense."

"Okay, well, if you see felt-tip pens - buy it, the children are buzzing at my ears. Sometimes they sell those things at the local market."

Karatai promised to look and left the house.

Cold western winds covered the road with dry, strong snow, which had been falling for the second day without ceasing. Turgat stood looking out at the snow, waiting for Karatai to leave the house.

"With how it is no one will ever be able to get here,"

Karatai remarked, glancing at the frequent crossings.

"Yeah, there is practically no road. An all-terrain vehicle is waiting for us at the central estate. At night I spoke with the director, perhaps he cleared the road?" Turgat, wanting to show his efficiency, spoke deliberately and precisely "While one hundred and forty sheep fell at four shepherds. In some departments they're still counting the death of their cattle."

"Who has the most losses?"

"Some shepherd in Burgrieden. Remember last year he came to us? He is about fifty years old, such a big man. He has seven children."

"I remember, I remember," Karatai said. "There was a guy like that..."

"He's bald."

"That I did not know. He did not take off his hat in the district committee." Karatai grinned, followed by the chauffeur and Turgat.

"They are interesting people," Turgat said, wanting to show that he knew each of the shepherds well. "Good workers, but, being in the district committee, they do not even guess to remove their little hats."

Two hours later they reached the central estate of the state farm. At the top of the hill, which stood on the border of the state farm, the director and chief specialists were waiting for them.

"Cattle are dying out there, and you are sitting at home," Karatai said, greeting them coldly.

"We are meeting with you..." the director began making excuses, but Karatai interrupted him.

"Why did you bring whole office? What, you have nothing to do?"

"Karatai Isaevich, we wanted you to see that everyone is here in place."

"Their place is where their cattle are dying!" he said, waving his hand to the stormy steppe. "You alone are enough for me. Is there a clear road somewhere here?"

"There is. Two graders came and cleared it at night."

"At night? Is this after they knew I was coming? It means that even yesterday the shepherds were cut off from the world. How did you communicate with them? What, did you get helicopters to pick them up?!

"Karatai Isaevich, we are not sitting idly by. All of the equipment is on snow retention. Graders had to be brought in from there..."

Karatai looked hard at the director and his subordinates, who were waiting with obvious fear to see how this conversation would end.

"The cattle depot has been built, but where do we get the boards for the poultry farm? From the stockyard! Volodya, give me a magazine!"

Karatai's driver, a Russian guy who knew the Kazakh language perfectly, pulled out the republican satirical magazine "Shmel" from the inner pocket of his sheepskin coat, and showed the director a caricature of the foreman's conversation with the heads of the economy.

"Look here!" Karatai said. "And you're actually living like this. The equipment given to you for field work, you use to clear the road. It's necessary to allocate a special, proper grader for this kind of thing! Or do you not know that there are drifts in these parts? Anyway, we'll talk more later. Go."

The management exchanged glances with indecision, and finally all eyes settled on the director at the same time, and he spoke cautiously:

"Karatai Isaevich, we would like to rest after journey here... The wife of one of the workers gave birth to a son yesterday... I would like to celebrate this event with you in our house."

Karatai looked straight at the director:

"A worker's wife gave birth to a son. Why should we celebrate this in your home?"

"We agreed to do so... Karatai Isaevich!"

Karatai found it funny to watch the director fuss, but he restrained himself. Not wanting to offend the worker in question, whose wife gave birth to a son; he looked softly at the red-cheeked man with amused eyes.

"Congratulations!" he said. "If there is time, we will sit at the table together, but if not..."

He almost said: "I'll take my share and go," but stopped in time. Somehow, going round the farms, Karatai ended up on that one. When he got there, he was in a hurry to leave, but how can the first secretary of the district committee up and go so carelessly? In order to somehow console the owner of the house and the director, he said something that almost flew off his lips. Coming out of the state farm office, he could clearly see that a load of ceremonial clothes was stuffed inside his car, it looked more like market stand than it did a vehicle. Karatai's hair stood on end.

"What is it?!" he asked the director, who was standing next to him.

"There are two nines," he grinned.

"What? What nines?"

"You are the most respected guest here at the celebration after all. Two pieces from each of the nine workers – that's eighteen chapans (ceremonial coat) we left in your honour." The director looked at him proudly, as if he had done a great public deed.

Karatai silently returned to the office, calling the driver behind him, and ordered him to put all the gifts on the table. At parting, Karatai told him:

"Do you know what will happen to you if I report this?"

The director's eyes popped out. He knew he had been caught trying to win over the secretary's favour.

"That's right," remarked Karatai, looking at the director for a long time. "This better not happen again!"

The director obviously realised belatedly how these gifts could be the end for him. By syllables and with great anguish, he squeezed out of himself a: "Goodbye!"

Since then, Karatai has been afraid to repeat that

same banal joke.

He took the director into his car, and they drove to the winter hut. Understanding the mood of the secretary, the specialists of the state farm disappeared somewhere.

The road that pierced by a grader at night, was already powdered with snow, and the Volga moved with an effort. The frost and wind here were much harsher than in the regional centre. The wipers worked hard, but still did not have time to brush off the snow from the windshield, and the road would either show clearly, or disappeared in a snowy shroud without a moment's notice. The Volga kept falling into invisible potholes, and the shaking made Karatai's head spin.

"Looks like the grader left the old, compacted snow here," Volodya remarked.

Halfway through, they saw one of the two graders standing dead in the middle of the steppe. Deciding that there was no one inside, Volodya managed to drive around them, but then they saw someone fussing inside, leaning their face against the glass, and Karatai, having stopped the car, went out onto the road.

The grader's driver poked his huge curly head out of the grader cab. His face turned blue from the cold; his thick, horse-like lips began to move.

"Oh, good sir, what are you doing here?" Karatai asked, ahead of the director, who again somehow began to fuss about petty things.

"What am I doing here? I'm guarding this here coffin," he blurted out.

"Why isn't your partner helping you?"

"Oh, how can he help me! I told him not to waste time on me. Now he is probably already near Burgenda."

A smile formed on the tired, exhausted, sleepless, frosted face of the horseman. The director of the state farm was scared to death because the machine operator was so rude and was so simply talking to the head of the district.

"Hey, don't act all important, get down from there!" shouted the director, shaking his fist from behind Karatai's back.

The man did not even pay attention to the threats, he calmly looked at the director, as if he were an empty place.

"I'm not used to walking around idly, why the hell should I get down," he said, frightening the director even more.

"Karatai Isaevich, do not pay attention to him!" the director was alarmed. "Hey, you haven't been drinking, have you? How is your speech?"

"Why, I already told you..." The horseman pulled out his flat nose deafeningly. "I said, the grader is barely alive, it can stand in the middle of the road, but that's about it. So no, I haven't, I was told to 'lie down like a corpse if you must but be there.' Here I am lying dead!"

The frankness of the machine operator to the head of the district infuriated the director. If they were alone, he would have shown him what was happening, but Karatai was present here, and the director was silent, ready to burst with anger. "Okay, we'll talk tomorrow," the director was angry.

"Since your coffin is broken, why sit in it, why didn't you leave with your friend?" said Karatai, not hiding his sympathy for the horseman.

"He went forward immediately; he has a stronger grader. I told him if I stop, that he shouldn't delay, time is precious after all. On his way back, he will definitely pick me up."

The director of the state farm did not like that the first secretary was so attached to some tractor driver and was trying to find out something from him. It seemed to him that Karatai wanted to leave a good impression of himself with an ordinary hard worker.

When the conversation seemed to be over and it was possible to go further, Karatai suddenly asked:

"Hey, sir, you look like a real hero. What size are your shoes?"

From such an unexpected question, both the director, and Turgat, and the grader driver, who had already settled down in the "heavens", were taken aback. But the question had been asked and had to be answered.

"How do I say it..." the man sniffed again. "My size is forty-three, but I wear that I can get my hands on..."

Karatai, suspecting something, looked at him searchingly:

"Show me your legs!" The grader was confused.

"Why? Here…" He stuck his right leg out of the cockpit.

"Come on and the other!"

"According to Sharia, putting your left foot in front of a person is not allowed."

"Hmm, you say it's not allowed according to Sharia?! I see how it is. Volodya!" Karatai shouted to the driver. "Come here…! How many kilograms can you lift?"

"On the bar, about a hundred, and on my back about a hundred and fifty kilograms, but not for very long," Volodya laughed.

"Then take this horseman off the grader and put him in our car."

Not understanding whether Karatai was joking or speaking seriously, Volodya first looked at his boss, then at the horseman, who was cheerfully grinning from above.

"Look out, make sure you don't drop him." The hefty horseman was all ready to perch on the back of the driver.

"Karatai Isaevich, are you serious?!" The director had completely lost his head and was already not far from turning his back. "Oh my god, what is this!" he exclaimed, seeing that Volodya had turned his back to the grader. "Where are you going! This is a joke," he yelled at the driver.

"It's not a joke!" Karatai snapped as he opened the car door.

Suddenly, the director's face turned pale. He saw how the left leg of the man sitting on Volodya's back dragged along the ground.

They drove in silence for a long time. This whole situation with the grader driver drove the director into a dead end, he literally lost his tongue. Clinging to each other with Turgat, they sat with bated breath. On top of that, the grader driver seemed to be pleased that he had frostbite on his leg just in time for the arrival of the authorities. He freely settled down in the back seat, squeezing the director to the door... "Those bastards, you need to answer for them," the director thought, angry. "If they freeze their leg, fall into a precipice, freeze in the cold after having too much booze – you are the one who had to answer for that. Damn, and they know it well! As if their life is needed not for themselves, but for others! Yes, I'm not cold and not hot, but if you're going to do something like this, at least freeze your head off next time! Well, they will punish me, well, they will remove me from my post. What's wrong with them?! Like if I get reprimanded, will his leg suddenly feel better? And how can an adult horseman even freeze his leg like that? Last winter, two shepherds got lost in a snowstorm, they were found three days later - and nothing happened to them. Only one of them had only two fingers frostbitten, and that because of their childishness, their youth. And this one, sitting in a tractor, loses a leg. Fell asleep, apparently. Got drunk and then fell asleep!"

He glanced at the grader driver. He, having closed his eyes in a sweet slumber, warmed himself in a warm cabin on a soft seat. Before putting the man into the car, Volodya rubbed his left leg with snow, and, probably, it must have helped a bit. The man slept without any signs of suffering.

"Well, good sir, what is your name? Who are you? Tell us," Karatai asked, turning to him.

The man opened his eyes and, as if asking, "Are you asking me?", lay silently for several seconds, reluctantly parting with drowsiness.

"Kenzhetai Orazov," he said quietly. "I am the last from my father, that's why they called me Kenzhetai, which means the youngest, the last... But on the other hand, the largest and tallest."

"So, you're healthy, but with frostbitten leg. Are you not ashamed?" Said Karatai, looking at the "youngest" with a smile.

"It was Allah who punished me for relying too much on my physique. I gave my best boots to one horseman, and my father took the others when he went to gather saxaul. So I had to stay in these worn-out boots. Interestingly, it hurt a bit at first, and then – after I got a little cut – there was no problem!" He looked amiably at the enraged director.

"That's all good if it passes, but if it doesn't, you will

remain disabled," Turgat intervened in the conversation.

"Ah," the man lightly waved his hand. "I've lived for twenty-nine years unharmed, and that's good enough for me. There are those who, as soon as they see the light, close their eyes and let it take them... My father had six kids, but in the end only two remained. All the rest disappeared from the very beginning!" He whistled for persuasiveness and went back to dozing.

From such a manner of talking to the authorities, the director's heart ached.

"Kenzhetai, stop saying the first thing that comes in your head! There are big people next to you!" he growled, not hiding the threat.

"I'm not talking about anyone; I'm talking about myself. But if I can't, I guess I'll be silent," he answered and fell silent with pleasure, instantly falling asleep.

Karatai looked at the guy with even greater interest and saw a book behind the lapel of his sheepskin coat.

"You are a brave person if you read under these conditions. What book do you have?"

Kenzhetai fidgeted with displeasure and took out a book from his bosom.

"I've read it twice. Here, I took it with me, I decided, if I have time, I will look through it again. I don't understand him. The writer is only two years older than me, yet why does he have such thoughts?!"

Karatai took the book, dishevelled, with a stained cover. It contained a photograph of the author. Cold, sharp eyes, piercing through and through, looked directly at him. Where the hell has he see him before? Oh, who cares where he saw him, he probably talked with this man at some point, and Karatai was ready to bet that their meeting was unpleasant.

Suddenly his heart fluttered. It's him! This is the man that Bagila told him about. The one he threw him out of the compartment!

He looked at the name of the author of the book. Jasyn Madiev. "What a coincidence!" Karatai thought. "I've only met him in difficult circumstances."

He leafed through the book and returned it to the man.

"When I have time, I will read it."

"You often sit at meetings don't you. Read it there," the man advised.

Karatai involuntarily laughed. The director, having heard such sedition from the lips of the grader, firmly decided to eradicate him from this world. Turgat had long been jealous of the secretary's attention on grader's operator and was offended that his boss had completely forgotten about him.

By lunchtime they had reached Burgenda.

As if wanting to see the worker arrive along the road he had laid, the second grader stood near a shepherd's hut, facing them with its frosty cab windows. As soon as they arrived, the shepherd, his wife and children poured out into the cold. Seeing that Kenzhetai was being carried in a stranger's arms, they froze in fear, and the second grader driver, thinking something bad had happened, rushed to his friend, but seeing that he was alive, and even smiling with pleasure, he exclaimed with admiration: "Oh you…!" and picked him up and put him on his back. The shepherd's wife, who had been standing like a pillar in one place all this time, only now breathed a sigh of relief, as if she had thrown a millstone off her back.

"Wow! Here I thought that Zhamankara's foal had died, but it turns out that it was a man!

"So are you happy or sorry that it's a man?" Karatai asked, stepping forward to greet her.

"Oh, I'm just glad they're alive, whoever it is! Is the chief from the district committee with you?"

Fearing that this one would say god knows what, the director of the state farm immediately intervened in the conversation.

"Are you blind? That's him, that's Karatai himself! And what about me, do you know who I am?!"

"God! Really?!" The woman pinched her cheek. "Hey, Kulzira, call everyone! Fast!"

Having received the order, the girl in a huge jersey and huge boots, gazing at the guests from under her brows, rushed towards a distant shed. The skirts of the jersey thumped on the tops of the boots.

"So, hello everyone! Otbai, this is our director, I did not recognize him, forgive me lord. Please do not be offended dear," she said, like an old person, although she and the director were around the same age. "This blizzard has completely tortured us, how many days it has been blowing. Well, come into the house. The bulldozer had just informed us of your arrival not long ago. The house is not cleaned... We weren't expecting anyone; the owner should be here at the moment..."

Karatai thanked the woman with a smile for her hospitality and said that it was not at all necessary to enter the house, they had business to attend to, but the hostess reared like an unleashed mare.

"I understand you are the authorities, but bread and salt matters above all!" she exclaimed indignantly. "If you came here to scold, then scold whilst sitting in your places of honour, we will listen, doing business by the hearth. I'm sure everybody has scolded our shepherd by this point, we are used to it!" There was a vicious character and some familiar malice in her voice. "Even our own children scold us, so we got used to it. Come in! You must be angry that we lost forty sheep. It's nothing, the state will not get poorer from this. Good is earned by a person. We have been grazing cattle for seventeen years. Over the years, we have raised not forty, but forty thousand sheep. And no one patted us on the shoulder, everybody just wags their fingers! They pay money, but no one will spare our children even a word. From birth, we have lived in this wilderness, away from people. Because of these forty fallen sheep…! Last year they swooped down at us like wolves..."

"Woman, that's enough! Shut your mouth! You'll work this out another time," the director sharply laid siege to the woman. "Karatai Isaevich, let's look into the house. It would be nice to warm up, drink some tea."

Silently listening to the hostess, Karatai looked at the director of the state farm and thought that there was apparently a lot going on here that he should have known.

When they entered the "living room" of the two-room adobe hut, two girls stretched out by the stove, as if on cue, one was seven, the other was four years old. The grader drivers settled behind the stove. Kenzhetai's partner provided medical assistance to his comrade. It was clear that the victim would have joked further on his deathbed, because when his partner hurt him, instead calling out for his "mother", he instead shouted out "father".

"God, when will they start to think! You can keep the house clean yourselves," the hostess shouted from the threshold. "Lay down the blankets. Can't you see we have guests? They always have to be reminded, they themselves don't understand a damn thing."

With a common effort, the girls pulled three blankets from a chest: one was laid on the torus, the other two along the walls. The smaller girl turned out to be surprisingly nimble, she energetically moved around the dwelling, her black hair covered her face every now and then, and she, like an adult, threw it back with her hand on the back of her head.

They laid the blankets neatly, smoothed them out, and sat down sedately in their places by the stove again.

"Four boys and three girls," said the landlady, whose name was Tenge, picking up the children's things scattered on the floor. "Two of the boys are at school, the other two with their father. This one, the oldest of the girls, just started going to first grade this year. She came here for the holidays, but she couldn't go back, everything if flooded over there. Now she has ride on the bulldozer to get back. It's good that you've come."

Tenge spoke of the bulldozer as if it were a person. According to her, it turned out that it can move on its own, and the driver, who was sitting behind the stove, had nothing to do with it. Karatai, noticing this, smiled slightly and thought that the sincere woman was not at all interested in the purpose of their arrival, but simply rejoiced at the guests.

When the guests were seated, Tenge said:

"Hey, Sopia, Maria, stop standing there like statues, serve tea!"

The girls were not forced to move twice, they quickly rushed to the samovar in the corridor.

"One of them has a Russian name, Maria?" Karatai asked.

"Maybe, who knows," Tenge answered, preparing a large black cauldron for the meat. "These names were given to them by my old man, he is completely out of his mind. He's as dark as the closet, and he climbs in there to read books as well, so he ended up scraping out the names of his daughters from there. It's as they say: there were once two women: one was in accounting, and the other was either in a chemistry or in physics. So, the old man gave his daughters their names. Over there on the window is the notebook, in which the gain and loss of sheep are marked, there are a dozen or two such names. Preparing them for future daughters." Tenge chuckled mischievously. "Would a normal person do such a thing!"

Everyone in the house laughed at that. Tenge, having amused the guests, grabbed an iron spoon and rushed to scrape the bottom of the cauldron, raising a shrill rattle in the room. The director sat with his brow furrowed.

"Oh, Tenge, stop that noise. We're fine without meat…" he muttered.

"What, you don't like it?" Tenge asked, peering out from behind the cauldron. "Okay, now I'll take it out into the street, I'll clean it there. You know, my old man loves it! When he is free and has nothing to do, he asks: 'Hey, clean the cauldron with an iron spoon.' So I scrape away. And he will listen, fall asleep and start snoring. All of the children leave the house at once and run for the hills."

"It turns out your old man is quite special!" Turgat giggled. "He's been gone for a long time."

"You saw him last year; he hasn't changed a bit since then..."

The fact that she addressed everyone so formally, namely him, offended Turgat to the point that he blushed with indignation.

Soon Kolbai appeared, becoming the subject of general conversation. Together with him, a huge cloud of frosty steam burst inside, in which the owner was consumed by for a moment, like in a fairy tale. Having emerged from this cloud, Kolbai stared at the guests with intense attention. He said hello, barely moving his lips, and silently settled himself at the very door he entered from. From his gloomy face, from his weak, indecisive look, it was not difficult to guess that things were not going well.

"What are the losses looking like?" Karatai asked bluntly as soon as the host and guests greeted each other. "There are forty now, five more recently fell," the shepherd muttered wearily.

Silence settled in the room.

"What's the matter?"

This question Karatai tormented the director the most. Inwardly shuddering, he waited for what Kolbai would say, and for some reason looked at the front door.

"In what...? There are many reasons. I can't say from the top of my head..."

"Name the main ones!"

Kolbai could not say anything intelligible for a long

time. He well understood that if he spilled the whole truth, he would be putting the director in the crosshairs in front of the none other than the secretary and make himself into such an enemy that even god forbids. But the first secretary silently waited for an answer, and the shepherd was forced to squeeze out:

"Today the cattle went into the winter thinner than usual. Also, the shearing was done too late..."

"That's your fault," Karatai cut him off. "Are there any other reasons?"

"What other reasons are there...? It's all my own fault. We, Kazakhs, are used to sacrificing our lives for the sake of livestock, so I'll serve my time for this blunder..."

Karatai realised that the shepherd's obedience was due not to his real guilt, but to something else, which he, the first secretary, did not know and, perhaps, would never know.

"If there are no other reasons, sit down," Karatai remarked and deliberately continued with cold indifference: "But don't think that they will put you in jail without asking anything."

"Turns out that it is not that easy to get into prison!" The shepherd joked sadly. "For seventeen years I kneaded the mud, froze my feet in the snow, forgetting about all the joys of life, I looked after the cattle. My family, children crawled behind me across the steppe... And in the end – I'm going to prison? You should frighten all the masters!" He began to speak and did not stop, looking at the fire raging in the furnace, not realising that his wife was looking at him with panic and fear. "So, I'll get forty-five from my own cattle, personally. The state gave me as a gift for my work. After that, you can take the rest of your flock! And I will go to the central estate, I will live quietly, without the wolves howling behind my back. I don't understand why we wander the desert steppe. Our hearts almost break with joy if we manage to see a living person during the whole winter. And now you show and say – 'prison!' I'm tired of it all! I'll leave!" He plucked a tuft of wool from the bedding beneath him and threw it into the oven.

"Kolbai, what is the matter with you? You can talk, but don't go off on tangents like that!" The director challenged him.

Kolbai abruptly raised his head, shot him with his eyes. Rage choked him, and the whites of his eyes were filled with blood. The director of the state farm wilted, unable to bear this silent duel.

"Don't like what I'm saying? Strong words were invented by the people, which means they are needed!" Kolbai flared up, unable to contain his anger. "As long as I have lived, not once had cattle fell in my flock, so not only a person, but also Allah himself will forgive me for using strong words. Do you want me to be polite? But how can I be polite if I end up disappearing for nothing? It's you, you drove me to this!"

The director was furious. He immediately realised that this half-wit would put all the blame for their deaths on him. He looked at Kolbai threateningly.

"Well, why did you stop?! Spread everything in front of our distinguished guest! What is my fault? That your frozen sheep die like flies from the slightest wind?" The director, who was lying on his side, raised his head and looked angrily at the owner with the air of a man demanding immediate justice.

"Is that how it is?" The shepherd breathed heavily. "Well, hold on! Who was it, that gave me weedy pastures during summer grazing? You! Who sent the fattest sheep to be butchered for a feast? You again! Who promised me ten stacks of feed? You! And what did you give me? Only one stack, and one that is farther from me than Mecca. Deceiving me by promising a tractor? That you did. Only recently did I see the equipment for the first time in the winter, and then they brought it for the sake of the district committee to pave the road. What other reasons were needed? And the cattle, therefore, should not fall, but give two lambs from each ewe? But wait, the worst is yet to come in spring, it's all just flowers, isn't it?! It'll be great if we save fifty out of a hundred lambs!"

Having shouted all this, Kolbai turned to the door, as if saying with all his appearance: "Now do what you want with me!" Karatai looked inquiringly at the director, then at Turgat, they were thinking, "Why are you looking this way!" None of them could immediately answer the secretary, and what was there to say. Turgat, trying to take the trouble away from himself, began to mutter that he travelled around with the director of his household, pointed out to him the shortcomings, which, due to remoteness, had to be controlled by phone. Karatai just shook his head, frowned, and waved Turgat away as if he were an annoying fly. He fell silent in mid-sentence, buried himself in a bowl of tea.

Karatai decided upon his arrival in the region to invite the directors of weak farms and talk to them properly. He considered it inappropriate to start this conversation with the director now, in the house of an already upset shepherd. He heard the most important thing: the secret words of the breeder, we let him grab onto the end of the disturbing thread leading to the truth, now it will not be difficult to get to that point himself.

"Today, forty-five fallen sheep were cleared off the list of the central estate. If you calculate how much it all costs, then the price will not exceed the loss of livestock," Kolbai spoke again on a hot topic. "Since there are roads, you must deliver the promised feed here."

"We'll deliver, we'll deliver," the director frequented, rejoicing that the shepherd was becoming more accommodating. "I'll go back to the state farm and find the culprits. I know there is plenty of food."

"What are we going to do with the dead cattle? Write up a report?" The shepherd looked askance at the director.

"We'll see... We need to consult with the veterinary service. Do you think the rest of the cattle will survive?"

"Who knows. The livestock barn seems to have been patched up. By evening, three or four wagons of hay will supposedly be brought up here. Now, after all, there is nowhere for the cattle to graze, there is so much snow piled up."

The conversation, having boiled over, flowed along a more even channel, and the hostess spread the food around with special pleasure. The girls tirelessly helped their mother. When the samovar was brought in and tea was poured, Volodya entered the house. In his hands he held a large bowl, in which dressed legs and a head of a ram lay perfectly.

"Master, where should I put this?" he asked as matter-of-factly as if he were one of the family members.

"What do you mean where? What, is there no room here?" Tenge challenged him. "If you can't see it yourself then just stand and hold it in your hands!"

Volodya realised that Tenge was saying this exclusively in her own way. He placed the bowl on a small table by the stove and sat down to drink tea.

"Lady, did you decide to bring the number of lost cattle to forty-six?" Karatai asked with a smile, watching Tenge putting meat into the cauldron.

"No, the number of the fallen will remain the same. This is my ram! All of the state sheep are thin, but mine are well-fed, a real Kazakh ram. Why should I serve you skinny meat?"

"Sorry we're in a hurry. We still need to visit some flocks; you started all this in vain." Karatai pointed to the dressed table, but the owner of the house did not even listen to him.

"The ram is intended for you, so you will have to taste the meat. After all, it's not like you see me every day?" The owner, satisfied, laughed. "Not every year I get an opportunity like this, who knows when I'll see you again!

Everyone around the table laughed with undisguised pleasure.

"And it's good to be around ordinary people," Karatai thought. "What can I say! They will all endure; they will all endure! And they might swear and curse at each other, whip each other with obscenities. But these people always have kindness and forgiveness... "

He had previously seen the owner of the house, who, seated at the door, drank his tea intently. Kolbai, like no one else, had the right to be offended by him, he had the right to say that he could help the ordinary shepherd, but does not wish to do so. But Kolbai kept silent, on the contrary, having slaughtered the ram, he pretended that all his worries were the little things in life, and most importantly, to show great Kazakh hospitality.

Last year, his younger brother was prosecuted, and Kolbai went to Karatai to ask for help. The brother, together with two horsemen were getting ready to see the female students at the neighbouring state farm. It was the hottest harvest time. There was about a ton of grain left in the onboard machine, on which Kolbai's brother worked - the combine broke down, and the brother was too lazy to go anywhere with such a small load. Right from the field, while technical assistance was repairing the harvester, they went to see some women. Leaving his friends at the women's hostel, he drove back to his field. On the highway, he was stopped by a raid detachment of the OBKhSS. Seeing the grain in the back, the police drew up an act. No one believed him, that he would never even think about stealing grain. During the investigation, it became clear to the horseman that he could be imprisoned for a year. It was then that Kolbai went to Karatai. "I can't put pressure on the court. Let him get justice," he said and almost kicked the shepherd out of his office. The people then explained for a long time, referring even to the district prosecutor, that the horseman was imprisoned for nothing.

If Karatai intervened in the case, the district court, of course, would listen to him. Then he regretted and scolded himself for a long time: looks like he found where to show integrity. He rode home with a feeling of awkwardness, he did not lift a finger to help the man, and now he had burst into his house and sat down in the most honourable place. But Kolbai pretended that absolutely nothing had happened, that the year that his younger brother had served was a mere trifle between them...

Karatai was at the table, and when Kolbai showed him his household, he tried to ask him about his brother, but each time he did not have the courage to start this conversation.

Two hours later he said goodbye to the shepherd's family. The healthy grader driver did not leave his frozen partner for a minute and finally brought him along. At the table, everyone was happy that the guy's leg came back to life. Having fed the patient, the comrade wrapped him in a warm blanket, put him in his grader, and drove ahead of everyone to the central estate. Saying goodbye to Karatai, the horseman suddenly said to him:

"Thank god you are our secretary. You are a kind and smart person. I'm sorry for any trouble we caused you. Goodbye."

"What are you talking about, just go!" The director shouted at the guy, but Karatai stopped him with a movement of his head and warmly said goodbye to the horseman.

Karatai took Kolbai's daughter with him to the district centre, who until that day could not go back to school. Seeing them off, the entire Kolbai family came out of the hut. The youngest cried so bitterly, as if her sister was being taken away in captivity.

The shepherd's lonely house quickly disappeared into a cloud of snow. Karatai suddenly felt sad, as if he had lost his way in the boundless steppe littered with snow. He was not accustomed to such weaknesses and with surprise undertook to look for the cause of this unaccountable acute anguish but could not find anything....

Karatai got home in the second half of the night. The wife quickly, as if she had not slept, opened the door, helped him to undress, out of habit, clearly reported who called, what news there was for the day.

He drank a cup of camel milk, looked at his sleeping children, and got into bed. But no matter how much he closed his eyes, he just couldn't fall asleep. For the umpteenth time, he began to think about the shepherd and his family. There, in this wilderness, in the middle of a blizzard, there was a lonely house. And all seventeen years, day after day, they are there in the snow. The shepherd's children grew up quickly, and they're completely different to his own. Where did their childishness go... It was clear that the snowstorms and dry winds blew everything away. There is maturity in their eyes, what strong words! And how pure and simple-hearted they are! And their parents are simple and trusting. They are ready to forgive everything. All seventeen years they did not ask anything from anyone, they themselves fussed about themselves and about the cattle. Of course, they are not the very first, but they work honestly, to the best of their ability. The main thing is that they will not deceive; they will not dishonour themselves. After all, the essence of a person can be recognised by their eyes. And in the eyes of Kolbai and Tenge there is no dishonour. This quality had passed to their children, the conscience will forever remain and will be the property of their family. And he scared Kolbai with a consequence! What a fool! Karatai scolded himself. How many thousands of sheep did the shepherd raise over the years? Why do we forget about it? He looked at his watch, it was three in the morning. He had to get up after four hours.

Karatai closed his eyes again. "Enough, you need to sleep a little, there is work tomorrow. What a life, there is no time to think calmly! What was his name? Madiev?" Karatai remembered the grader's book and immediately the conversation with his daughter in the mountains came back to him. And Sargel's letter... It all has something to do with it. "Why did Bagila tell me about this man? Just to remind me how I got him out of the compartment? Just for this? No... It's not that simple."

"What are you thinking about?" Asked his wife, seeing that he was awake.

"Yes, so." Karatai evaded the answer. "I think we should go to Alma-Ata."

"What, again for the party meeting?"

Karatai chuckled.

"Yes, something like that. A family meeting."

In the spring, a new book by Jasyn came out. This was his third. The annotation said that the author seeks to show a bright image of our contemporaries in the story. Their love and devotion to their native land, the best and noble qualities of their soul, reflection on life and its problems. It was also reported that the language of the story is bright, original, the book is easy to read. Jasyn ran his eyes over these lines and swore in annoyance: "Damned publishers! They don't know any other words. What a love for stamps. Who would read a book with such an annotation!"

Surprisingly, the newspapers bypassed a deathly silence about the new book of the sensational prose writer, which came out after a three-year break. It was as if this book never existed, as if the author had not written anything - not a single review, not a single word in passing in review articles about literature. It turns out that his thoughts, the created images, his imagination and reflections, which took three years of his life, are not worth a single penny?!

He picked up the latest issue of the literary weekly. It contained a huge article about the last story of a writer, his age.

Jasyn read this story in manuscript, the author asked him to express his opinion. He didn't like the story. It's not enough to say he didn't like it, it was involved along-side small, insignificant events, the red price to pay to be but a note in the newspaper. From the first to the last page of the story, the young specialist, with the support of the party committee, fought in the economy to improve things, and finally he himself became the director of the state farm.

"God!" After reading the story, Jasyn really despaired. "Can this really be considered literature? He seems to be crazy! He probably still thinks that this is a new step in creativity. How can you suggest this to the reader? Our poor literature, what and whom only it does not tolerate! But he is waiting for praise... He also believes that he will be praised highly. Poor fellow, why is he writing?!"

Jasyn wrote a few lines, put the paper into the manuscript of the story, and left the house on the eve of the author's arrival, telling his wife to hand him the folder herself. The young writer came, expecting Jasyn's enthusiastic words... After reading his note, he froze, all pale, not knowing whether to believe what was written or not: "All this is office fiction! If you don't feel sorry for literature, then at least have pity on the readers."

"Ah! He thinks he's so smart! Time will tell which one of us is the fool! "Have pity on the readers"! If he is so compassionate, let him first stop writing his muddled stories! He himself only digs into the crap and brings back blackness. And when we write about a bright life, he immediately doesn't like it!"

"Say what you need to say, don't talk so much. A writer should be ashamed to talk like that!" said Jasyn's wife, frowning.

"How could he! And you, you sing the same songs as him. He thinks that there is no one left in literature besides him, and this is because two or three blockheads once praised him! Let's see how long he will remain at the top!"

"Talk to him about it! There is a sick father lying in other room, don't shout like that."

Jasyn's colleague slammed the door in parting.

A huge article, in which this story was assessed as a new stage in the development of literature, caused Jasyn to laugh. However, such outlandish things were not a surprise to him...

Criticism, which he forgot to even think about, hit the book about two months later and in that newspaper. No stone was left unturned from the book. Ideological vagueness, suspicious ambiguities, the characters are victims of their complexes, the plot does not correspond to the truth of life, language and concepts are alien to the Kazakhs, "creative stagnation…" The article consisted only of such expressions.

For Jasyn this was the strongest blow. Actually, not the criticism itself, but the deliberate murder of the book, entrusted to a not very smart person. He was painfully worried that the newspaper did not disdain this scribbling. For two days, Jasyn tried to write a rebuke to the criticism, but realising that by doing so he would get involved in a senseless skirmish, Jasyn abandoned the idea. "Why show character," he thought. "The writer must be criticised, and he must be ready for this. My goal is to write, to defend myself against fools – these kinds of arguments are not for me. And also, only the weak need to protect themselves, but for now I am confident in myself!

Two weeks later, he was kicked again in a youth newspaper. The article was called "Shadow on the Wattle Fence..."

On that same day he called Bagila.

"I'm at the hotel," he said, barely saying hello. "I'm sitting in a friend's room, we studied together. He left on a business trip, will be late in the evening. I'm waiting."

"Will we be together?"

"When will you stop being afraid of me? Like a real Kazakh, you are horrified by the word 'hotel.'"

"Yes. I will always be afraid of you."

She heard Jasyn chuckle.

"I promise I'm not scary all of the time. How soon can you be with me?"

Bagila thought about how long it would take her to travel, and then asked:

"Should I bring today's article?"

"No need. It's here in front of me. I'm in room five hundred and thirty."

"Okay, I'll be there in an hour."

It was the last days of May. Low-rise buildings were drowned in blooming lilacs and apple trees, only high-rise buildings broke out of the spring boil, reflecting the pink light of the evening sun on their marble walls. In the south, an icy horseshoe, trimmed with blue spruce forests, stood on the Alatau, proudly carrying its grandeur and eternal beauty.

Bagila was suddenly overwhelmed with joy. Waving a thick camel-hair sweater in her arms, she merrily ran up the stairs. Climbing up to the fifth floor, she went to the door numbered five hundred and thirty. Probably, he was waiting for her at the very doorstep: as soon as she knocked, Jasyn opened the door, instantly dragged her into the room, kissed both of her hands in turn.

"The horror!" Bagila exclaimed, looking at him and wincing. "It reeks of booze! Have you been drinking alone."

"Yes. Sometimes it's good to drink alone, without a drinking buddy."

"What's good about that? Turns out that you could not resist criticism, huh? This weakness doesn't really fit your character." Bagila said, throwing the sweater on the bed and settling herself in an armchair opposite Jasyn. "Are you sick by any chance? Your eyes don't look so good."

"No," Jasyn shook his head. "It is impossible for my eyes to be ablaze with fire."

"Yes, your affairs are apparently not going so well," said Bagila. "Why did you call me?"

"In honour of the criticism addressed to me."

"You know what…" Bagila looked straight at him. "Lika and I talked about you for a long time today. We talked for more than an hour… About your work, about your family, about these articles. Lika likes you very much. Today she literally cried because of this article. And just then uncle Sargel came in and began tormenting her with questions, he asked why she was crying. They quarrelled as usual, and in the end, she burst into tears for real. He still remembers that cigarette butt pretty well...

"I am so glad for them!" Jasyn smiled sarcastically.

"He just hinted at something to my dad. A month ago, dad came to me, and we talked about a lot. Previously, dad did not give me advice, but then he suddenly said: "Look, daughter, your misfortunes first echo in us, think about the honour of your parents and your own honour." It seems to me that he knows about you... After that conversation, I really became attached to him.

"Now he's trying to find a way to get rid of me again?"

She looked at Jasyn with curiosity, but he seemed to have already forgotten about her, he sat, busy with his thoughts, mechanically leafing through magazines. It was always like this when he had a difficult time: he became indifferently careless and coldly calm. Bagila, noticing this, tried not to ask unnecessary questions, realising that some important thought was ripening in him, and it was weightier than all of her words.

Jasyn opened the window. Cool air rushed into the room and with it the sound of a fountain beating in the square in front of the hotel. He looked for a long time at the opera house, whitening with columns opposite, at the people strolling decorously by the fountain. Bagila tried, but could not get used to Jasyn, when he became like this: withdrawn, detached, as if she was not around and never was.

"Sur, come here," Jasyn suddenly said without even looking in her direction.

Bagila nervously leaned back in her chair.

"Why should I come over?!" She even turned away with wounded pride.

"Well, please, your dignity will not suffer, I promise. Just come here."

With painful reluctance, she rose from her seat and stood beside him.

"Look how careless people are, how they rush to live. Somewhere there are wars, coup d'état, new states arise. Some people die, others are born... How many languages, how many customs, how many hopes and despairs. And none of us really know each other. For example, in Africa, not a single person realises that in the distant city of Almaty, in the five hundred and thirtieth room of this hotel, we are standing together, and you are terribly offended by my request to come to me, and that today in the newspaper I was criticised as the last graphomaniac. No one knows but the two of us. It's a pity!"

Bagila looked at him, not understanding what he was saying.

"What's a pity?!"

"It is a pity that the concept of "humanity" is so abstract. Somewhere on earth, two people, a she and a he, are madly in love with each other. They can't live apart, and people couldn't give a damn about that.

"Why do we need to know about them?"

"And no one knows us. Nobody!"

Bagila winced: after all, he is a weirdo!

"Why 'and us'?"

"We love each other after all."

Jasyn, continuing to look out the window, put his hand on her shoulder. Then he drew her to him, pressed him tightly with his right hand and kissed her temple. She felt dizzy, lord, can he really be so gentle and defenceless?! Bagila almost cried at this revelation.

He realised that this intimacy with her was the most unique, most sacred moment, the only one for him, and, god forbid, for her. Is this amazing feeling going to rumble for next couple of hours in his chest? Maybe for every single day? He turned Bagila towards him, looked straight into her eyes.

"Is that really true?" Jasyn asked, not at all understanding what was happening to him.

Bagila was silent. She did not know what to answer him, how could she talk about it... Sooner or later - she was waiting for this day - he had to open up to her, and that's all happened. Now she was terrified. Where, into what dead ends, will this magical attachment to him lead her? He has a wife, children, a settled life in which he is not at all free. What will come out of their closeness, secrets, furtive meetings in deserted corners, in hotel rooms? But without him, Bagila could no longer imagine life. From the time she got to know Jasyn, all the other guys began to seem flat and insipid to her. Every meeting with him was an event. Jasyn did not always give himself up without looking back to his mood and feelings. Sometimes he became unbearably scrupulous, wayward, he seemed to take pleasure in offending her. At such moments she hated him and looked for an excuse to leave as soon as possible. Already an hour after parting, Bagila reproached herself that she had left Jasyn alone, being offended like a child, and on the same day she called him.

"To tell you the truth, you don't look like a lyricist at all, and for god's sake, don't look at me like that. It is impossible to love a person with such a look. Besides, there is no need to ask whether we like each other or not." She burst into silvery laughter and returned to her chair.

"That's right," Jasyn squeezed out a semblance of a smile. "It is true that they say that a real student surpasses a teacher. Okay, let's finish the lyrical part here." He poured himself some wine. "I wanted to be myself today, but I see that nothing came of it. Indeed, we have forgotten how to talk about each other."

"Not at all. I never knew how to, and you, quite possibly, have only just forgotten."

"Bravo! I give you permission to do this!"

"I'm going to do this without your permission. And from this moment refer to you in an informal way. Lately, these formalities have been getting on my nerves. Hearing the way I talk to you, I'm immediately reminded of uncle Sargel, who always speaks to his wife formally."

"Wonderful. This is one more step towards our marriage." Bagila's cheeks flushed. She frowned seriously.

"We will never be husband and wife. And in my heart, I will always treat you informally."

Jasyn stood up, slowly approached her, imperiously took the glass from her, put it on the table and kissed her on the lips just as imperiously. When she jumped up, ready to fight back, he had already moved to the window. Bagila gasped at such impudence. She sank into a chair and wept softly.

"It's not fair. After all, you are a jerk!"

"I know," Jasyn agreed with complete indifference. "Let it be unfair, but it is also unfair that for three years I have never kissed you once. Even ashamed."

"Anyone can do that."

"Why shouldn't I be like everyone else?"

"I don't know... You are different for me. However, if you want..."

"Yes, today has not been a good day since early very morning," Jasyn thought wearily. "How much more trouble will there be before tonight?"

"Okay, sorry," he said caustically. "You can assume that I didn't kiss you. I take it back."

Bagila looked at him sharply. Jasyn noticed a spark of rage in her eyes.

"Do you think you said something smart?" She asked contemptuously, treating him formally again. "Quite the opposite. And in general, today it is better for you to be silent, the ability to speak has changed you."

Jasyn fidgeted in his chair, as if he was sitting on something sharp. Bagila hit him right where it matters.

"Yes!" he exclaimed in a cheerful voice. "I just thought today was a bad day. But what does a good day mean? This is when all your desires were fulfilled, every step was accurate. But sometimes luck does not give a person anything. We are to blame for everything. And what are you looking at? Yes, you are to blame as well! I had so many thoughts and I was going to post them today. It didn't work out. And it's good that it didn't work out. Since you have become attached to me, I do not know what and how to do things, the old confidence has betrayed me."

"Now I see! So, after I got attached to you! Now you're looking like yourself," Bagila laughed. "Nasty things suit you very much! How lovely!"

"Do I have to tease you all the time to please you? You seem to be terribly fond of playing with words!"

"You won't be able to piss me off today."

"Because you're still hungry for words, and I'm fed up with them."

"But you still talk!"

"Do you want me to shut up?! Hey, what was it again, Bagila... Ugh, what a stupid name you have. Listen, Sur, if you start arguing with me, I will kiss you again."

"Please!" Bagila raised the glass to her lips just in case.

"What?! What did you say!"

"Oh, the joy on your face! I said I didn't mind."

She seems to have completely confused Jasyn. "You just got offended, didn't you?"

"And what should I do about it, I realised that anything can be expected from you."

Jasyn was silent.

"Have you swallowed your tongue? Or are your brilliant thoughts dishevelled like feathers in the wind? However, it is better to remain silent than to carry on with any nonsense. This is below your dignity."

Jasyn approached her.

"Just don't tear the glass out of my hands," Bagila smiled somehow pathetically.

"Why the hell do I need it! Keep yourself healthy." Jasyn stroked her head. "You know, at such moments I don't want to be in love, like every other person, when love ends in bed. We must be a thousand times higher than that."

"Then we will become an Akhalteke and leave to roam the boundless land... Do you remember?"

"I remember. I'm ready right now. But what to do if

we remain human. Listen, is there a man in your family who has died of drunkenness? Put this glass on the table. It turns out that you are insatiable for words and for champagne."

Bagila almost choked.

"I haven't even had one glass."

"And that is a lot! I have a friend who gets drunk at the sight of a vodka cork. And you are a woman!"

"God, if my father or uncle Sargel had heard all this! They would have thought that I set out to dishonour our entire family, to give our family dignity to you for desecration. And I, it seems, will become even more pliable," she put the glass on the table. "Well, what should I do?"

"Nothing! I'm probably no worse than that unfortunate Czech glass. But the wine glass is directly stuck to your lips. Be quiet, don't laugh!"

Jasyn leaned over her and kissed her on the lips. Bagila closed her eyes... He suddenly smelled a sharp smell of perfume, felt the taste of her lipstick. He became disgusted. "They all smell the same. What is all this for," thought Jasyn, pulling away from Bagila.

She opened her eyes, and he saw how pride in her was replaced by modesty, waywardness - humility. And he read in her eyes: "We have crossed the border, what will happen next?" - "Will we go farther? A person cannot escape the laws of prescribed existence," he answered her to himself, realising that the girl would never ask him such a question out loud, and he would never answer it, would not be able to answer it.

"Your lipstick is of high quality. Despite the champagne you drank, it has not lost its taste on your lips," said Jasyn, so as not to be silent.

"Is this the first thing you think about after a kiss?"

"Yes, as long as no other problems concern me."

By his harsh tone, Bagila understood Jasyn's inner state. She already knew well that he talked about the little things when he wanted to hide his mental confusion from those around him.

"I almost forgot," Jasyn lit a cigarette somewhat hastily. "I just saw the artist who painted your portrait... Now he is painting another one."

Bagila raised her eyebrows in surprise when she heard that Jasyn knew about that portrait.

"How do you know this?"

"You yourself told me what he looks like. It's guy called Estay Imanov, a well-known portrait painter. One of the few artists I respect. He had two solo exhibitions. He's young. Talented."

"Oh my god, there are just too many talented people in this world!" She sighed softly, not daring to look at Jasyn.

"No, it's not like that," he retorted calmly. "Not everyone is gifted. There are amateurs - yes! But real talent is rare."

"Did he say he was painting a second portrait?"

"What's wrong with that? He has been watching

you for a long time."

Bagila's eyes widened.

"Oh my god! This is utter shamelessness! As if I don't have enough guys following me around!"

"He didn't follow you."

"What do you mean?"

"Simple. He simply follows the object of his future work of art. For him, you are not Bagila Karataevna, not a student of the Faculty of History, not the painful love of a writer broken in the newspapers, but just material - and nothing more."

"Thanks." The girl bit her lip in disgust. "Maybe you need me as material? Write your next story, after which I will also not be needed."

"You know it happens. In writing practice, even valuable material loses its significance over time."

The indifferent, calm answer of Jasyn threw Bagila into a rage.

"Rather than waiting for me to become irrelevant, it's better to leave of my own free will. I bet it will be right thing to do."

"Don't be scared, I don't write about love and beautiful girls. And then, for me you are not an object. I love to write about the ugly and the thin. They are smarter."

Bagila did not know how to react to these words: to be happy or to be offended.

"You know," she said, "you are like ice in a hot cauldron. Warm on one side, cold on the other."

Jasyn, amazed by such a comparison, carefully looked at Bagila and shook with laughter.

"Wonderful! Hope I don't melt?"

"Don't worry, I doubt it'll be a threat to you!" Still not freed from anger, she spoke loudly, as if whipping Jasyn with words. "And tell that guy, for god's sake, to stop sending his portraits to my home."

Jasyn chuckled condescendingly.

"It turns out that you have a primitive idea of art," he blew a puff of smoke towards the window. "In my opinion, this portrait will be a phenomenon in the painting world, and it is not painted in order for him to drag it to your house. This portrait will be exhibited at all exhibitions."

"He... last time he sent it to my house!" Exclaimed the girl, trembling with indignation.

"Yes, but it was just a sketch. Didn't you notice that?"

Bagila jumped up and ran out onto the balcony. Jasyn snorted dismissively: "It's nothing, it's not the first and it won't be the last time, as it flared up, it will cool down." But Bagel lingered too long on the balcony. "It looks like she was really offended. Shall I go and calm her down?"

He slowly approached her. The girl, as if forgetting where she was, looked at the people bellow, at the hissing jets of fountains. He coughed, reminding himself, and touched her shoulder guiltily. Bagila didn't even look in his direction.

Jasyn saw that she was crying. Tears glistened on her cheeks, reflecting the blue neon light of the streetlights.

"The woman is in tears," he said, looking over the faces of people below. "They emphasise your charms. I am afraid of women who never cry, they are usually cunning and two-faced. You know, now women all over the world are facing one problem - how to remain a woman!" He squinted at Bagila and thought: "how is she, is she still angry?"

She walked around him like a pillar, entered the room, nervously grabbed a jacket from the back of the chair.

"Yes, I don't know much and don't want to know! I lived happily without it!"

"You're right," he said to fill the void between them. "To know a lot is a disaster for women's happiness. He who knows little lives quietly and well..."

"You are a ruthless person! You have an answer for everything. There is no warmth in your heart at all."

"I'm looking at the truth, that's all. In the future, do not strive for knowledge, otherwise you will lose all your friends. People don't like it when you're taller than them."

Bagila pulled a handkerchief out of her purse.

"I wish I didn't know you!" She said angrily, but without the previous fury. "You scoff at my every word; it is pleasant for you to watch a person cry. You are twelve years older than me, and you act as if you were an equal opponent. You are married, you have children, and I'm here with you..." She said, choking on tears, after falling silent.

"Are you leaving?"

"Yes… What am I supposed to do here?!"

She carefully folded her handkerchief, closed her purse, clicked the clasp, slowly put on her sweater, obviously unhurriedly fastened the buttons. She waited for what Jasyn would say, but Jasyn, instead of reassuring her or detaining her, only said:

"Good luck." And, lighting a cigarette, he went to the open window.

"We won't meet again?"

"Maybe. If you need me, call me."

"Is this how it all ends? Why did all this happen? For what? Don't think that I'm sticking to you. I just want to understand why we dated for three years. In order to say nasty things to each other and run away?! And you…! After me, you will tie another girl to yourself and again you will be..."

Jasyn turned sharply to her. His face was painfully pale, his eyes shone feverishly.

"Yes, I will find, and I will tie!" He said as if he chopped something off, cold fury in his voice. "I have no other business! I came into existence only to explore the charms of girls. If you haven't been able to understand me in three years, then you'd better leave now. In six years, it will become completely unbearable, you will even regret that you did not immediately run away from me!"

Bagila trampled a little at the threshold and, without even waiting for a kind look or gesture from Jasyn, quietly left.

She didn't remember how she got home. As soon as the door to her room closed, Bagel burst into tears. And the more she cried, the more bitter despair rang in her. Never before had she been so confused and weak.

Malika was also crying: Without even asking what happened, as soon as Bagila threw herself on the bed, she burst into tears. Fearing that Sargel, sensitive as a magpie, might suspect something, Bagila found the strength to stop crying and lay down in bed, hoping to forget herself in a dream. The anger and despair subsided; she began to think calmly, soberly. And immediately Jasyn appeared before her eyes.

"He was left alone there," thought Bagila. "All alone. Or maybe he's all alone in life? Do not strive for knowledge - you will lose all your friends... Why did he say that? To whom? To me? What if he was talking about himself? God, how difficult it is for him. And to forget him... It's doubly difficult! How ruthless he is…! It can't be. Such people understand grief and know how to sympathise. A thinking person cannot be heartless. Or does he want to get rid of me? Who knows, he is tormented by a multitude of thoughts entangled with each other in contradictions. It's much harder for him than for me. A little harder. But what am I to do…? Where will he take me? After all, it's impossible, having lost your head, to follow him, I still don't know what he wants? Of course, he is special, not like others, he thinks, speaks differently than everyone else, but do I need such a life? Indeed, in fact, it may turn out to be alien and incomprehensible to me… I have my own life, my own ideas about it. Next to me live relatives, close ones, they love me, and I love them, in this life of mine, my parents, sisters. Let me think and live not as significantly as he does, but so what? This does not mean that I have to give up everything. But where will this ship take me? How will everything go on? Will I stay with him, or will I have to go back? Can I return on my own? What to do? Swim or get off? I must solve this, and quickly, this ship is moving away from my native coast."

Two days later, Malika and Bagila were talking, sitting on the balcony.

"All women are unhappy," Malika said, continuing to knit a children's sweater. "Because our life consists of participation in the sorrows and joys of others. We are much thinner than men, and we forgive them more often. It happens that we ourselves are not sweet, but we suffer for someone, shed tears."

"Lika, tell me, will I be happy?"

Malika, leaving her knitting, looked at Bagila, as if trying to understand what she wants to hear in response.

"I don't know… You want to subordinate everything

to reason."

"Is it bad?"

"Why? If anything, it's just too good!" Malika spoke diligently and clearly, like a student in a lesson. "Of course, there is nothing wrong with trying to be a good person." Bagila tried to look into Malika's eyes.

"You don't seem to be telling the whole truth."

"Me?" Malika made her eyes wide, her tone falsely surprised. "Why should I deceive you?"

"I do not know. You speak somehow evasively and too calmly. Why are you so addicted to knitting? It's still far away until winter, you will have time to knit this sweater."

Malika blushed as if caught in a lie, put down her knitting and began to speak, carefully hiding her eyes.

"To be honest, a thinking and understanding person cannot always be happy. After all, he spends all his strength and energy on the lives of others, but he himself has no time to live."

"Meaning..."

"What do you mean 'meaning...?' Maybe that really is happiness, judging by and large. And if on a personal note..." she shrugged, "you know, most good people are unhappy, but the most amazing thing is that they never consider themselves to be unhappy. I do not understand this..."

"Lika, you are somewhat thoughtful today, more than ever before. I only asked about myself..."

"And I'm only talking about you."

"So you're saying that by and large I am happy, but not personally? What kind of fluff is that?! And then, I do not consider myself unhappy."

"Maybe I'm not speaking clearly, but you have the makings of these qualities. Who knows what kind of life you have ahead of you. A person is changeable... People whom I considered sensual and subtle in my youth have now completely changed. Many of them became cunning, enterprising, and those whom I thought were blockheads turned out to be real people. Apparently, I don't understand people."

"Back then, at home," Bagila suddenly started up, "I wanted to finish school as soon as possible, to become an adult. The world was so beautiful, it seemed to me that all it needed was me to make all of humanity happy. And then all of a sudden, that was not the case."

She smiled slightly bitterly. She wanted to say a lot more: that, it turns out, life is actually quite different, that there is a lot of evil in it, but Bagel did not have enough words, and she also felt that it was hardly worth opening up like that now that Lika had pulled away from her. The fact that her Jasyn was kicked out of the compartment like a puppy, that she could easily get into the institute, and her friend, having passed her exams perfectly, did not find her last name among those enrolled, that the dark-haired one, having grabbed a deuce in history, became a student, Sargel's path to science, Malika's life - bright from the inside and dark in reality - vicious articles that shattered Jasyn's book to smithereens - all this quickly passed in a string in her mind.

"Yes, you are probably right..." She said, watching two kids in the yard pour water on each other from a toy bucket. "I already know that I will not forget this man, but his path... he has his own path."

"Sur." Malika finally dropped her knitting onto the windowsill. "It's a good thing that you said it yourself. Jasyn is a peculiar person, he is not yours. It may be hard to hear, but I will say that you need to forget about him. Will have to forget. Leave for the summer holidays somewhere far away, to the Black Sea, for example, or to Borovoye. Let's go together, huh?"

Bagila did not want to hear Lika say these words, and even so calmly, weightily. It felt like someone was holding her heart with a cold hand. And this was said by that Malika, who was so delighted with Jasyn, what happened to her? Why does she want to break up with Jasyn?

"Besides… your summer class is coming soon. Don't forget that you came to study! We are responsible for you to Karatai."

It seemed to Bagila that Malik was speaking to her at the prompting of Sargel. Those were his words, right and wrong, like a sweaty palm.

"Yes, the class is coming soon..."

She swallowed back her tears. Malik understood

this and grabbed the knitting again, as if her child was freezing and all the salvation was in that sweater.

Bagila looked at Malika for a long time, feeling irritation rise inside her towards this woman. Losing her self-control, she screamed at the top of her voice:

"Like, what's wrong with you? What are you hiding from me? For heaven's sake, stop knitting! What are we going to do in this Borovoye?!"

Malika took a deep breath. A pitiful expression appeared on her face, as if she were about to drink a bitter mixture.

"Sar is going to do something," she said lastly. "He wants to meet Jasyn. And you know how stupid and rude he is. I'm afraid that when he rushes to Jasyn, moving his Adam's apple, with bulging owl eyes, the noise will rise throughout the city. What will happen if Jasyn's wife finds out about everything? And not from a stranger, but from a relative of the girl?"

Bagila was scared. This fright instantly overshadowed all the insults inflicted by Jasyn.

She knew that sooner or later her relationship with Jasyn would cease to be a secret. Often, she dreamed of how she would tell her parents everything - and would talk about him joyfully, with a light and pure heart. Now all this will turn out quite differently. Riding the evil channel of some gossip.

"No, that's impossible!" cried Bagila. "How does he know? I won't let him meet Jasyn!"

"What can you do?"

"I'm leaving! Now, to another city! To another institution!"

"Don't be a fool," Malika besieged her, "Capital gossip will reach the new city with you or even before you. Besides, you will disgrace both us and your father.

"What should I do?"

"I'll explain everything to Sar myself. Let him just try and open his mouth. And in the summer, we will go to the Black Sea. Maybe you really will forget about it. Deal?"

Bagila wept, dropping her face into her hands,

On the evening of the same day, Sargel entered the house in a great mood. Climbing the stairs, he hummed to himself, and when he opened the door, he completely shocked Malika by holding out flowers to her, bowing gallantly at the same time.

"Today is our wedding day, remember?" He said, pulling off his sweaty hat.

"Ooh! Thank you!" Malika was sincerely amazed at her husband's act, but immediately forgot about him, admiring the flowers. "Sar, you don't know the difference between a broom and a bouquet. How did you manage to choose such a beauty?!"

"Men are an inexhaustible treasure! We have many advantages; you just need to be able to see them!" Sargel bared his teeth in a smile. "We will celebrate this event at home, we will not go anywhere. The birthday of the hearth should be celebrated at the very hearth."

Malika completely forgot what day it is today. And when Sargel handed her the flowers, she felt a ringing emptiness in her heart, there was neither joy nor excitement. And never will a living feeling, a marital passion appear in her heart, except sometimes a tear of despair will drip... Actually, she knew this very well before. But now Malika nevertheless pretended to be a devoted, loving woman, hugging her husband around his thin wrinkled neck. And she suddenly felt a little better. After talking with Bagila, the house needed at least some kind of, even if false, joy, and it arose through this.

An hour later everyone was at the table. Mancia and the children, who usually stayed in the kitchen at the time of feasts, were now in the room. Mancia, having settled herself comfortably, immediately buried herself in a book, so that they would quickly forget about her. Sargel decided to put the table in perfect order.

"Mancia, everything has its time, dear! We eat at the table, but do not read, just as they read at the desk, but do not eat."

"The one who can do pedagogy does it, the one who does not understand this science teaches others," she blurted out, smiling sarcastically.

Sargel's eyes popped out of their sockets for a second and returned to their proper place. Glancing over everyone with the eyes of the head of the dinner table, he turned his gaze personally to Mancia.

"This, too, is the result of over reading," he said, conciliatorily clear. Sargel didn't seem to want to part with his benevolent mood today. "If the acquired knowledge is not directed to the benefit of the cause, it turns into a corrupting poison for a person. Knowledge is like a hunting golden eagle. If the bird is released for nothing when there is no animal nearby, the golden eagle, angry, attacks the hunter himself. Such is the word! It often hits the owner. My tongue is my enemy!" Sargel raised his finger to the ceiling and laughed, snorting. He was pleased with his tirade. Mancia's eyes gleamed with rapacity. Noticing this, Sargel broke the silence, fearing that she would attack. "Soon you will finish your studies and will go in different directions. That's when you'll miss your uncle!" He perked up as he imagined how Bagila and Mancia would miss him. "You know how I long for my childhood, back when I had nothing but a torn shirt and a piece of bread. Oh, that's we need! And so, I want this childhood, albeit the hunger, to return even for a day! And you... What bad things did you see in my house? Nothing! Everything is here, there is prosperity in everything, no one refuses you anything! Well, there are, of course, misunderstandings, but they are transient, and you quickly forget about them. Let's raise this toast to Malika, who is a wife to one of us, an older sister to the others, and a third," he made a terrible expression and leaned towards the children, "-a mother!

To the dregs!" Sargel called out but was immediately surprised that all three female representatives briskly and completely overturned the wine.

After her husband, Malika started speaking.

"Today is a special day for me and Sargel. I want to say that in the hustle and bustle of our daily affairs, the day of creating a family hearth should not become dull and mundane. I ask you to drink for Sargel, who is close to each of us! To the dregs!"

She skilfully emptied her glass. Mancia and Bagila did not lag behind her. Sargel's eyes darted across them with a peculiar gleam. Sargel then pursed his lips and pressed them together, keeping out the anxious thoughts that instantly flared in his doctor head.

But still suspicious... He wanted to celebrate the day of his legal marriage with Malika with a warm home-made dinner, and not with such a swift drink. Sargel was greatly frightened when he saw how his ladies properly kissed the wine glasses. "Where is that coming out? So, they can drink? Where did they learn? Somewhere else. Maybe they are smoking cigarettes there with might and main."

He looked searchingly at his wife, Mancia and Karatai's daughter. Look, such calm faces! Just pure innocence! And if you offer them anything - they will just stun another glass. Sargel spelled out his wife's toast in his head. "She lies all over, mocks me, smiles with some kind of overtones..."

An hour later, Sargel dismissed the feast.

"Listen, Sar," Malika said to him when he came into the kitchen to watch his wife wash the dishes and leaf through the newspaper. "I'm glad about your idea to celebrate your wedding day. Honestly! But admit it, besides this, you have some other news. Why are you so silent?"

Sargel sedately put down the newspaper, chuckled, as if to say: "Oh, you are cunning!"

"Yes, there is more!" he began, and all his doubts crushed his joy and complacency.

Malika, ready to hear something unusual, froze with a wet plate in her hands. Sargel did not want to tell just like that, right away, he paused with pleasure, put on a face a dignified expression. Apparently deciding that the atmosphere already corresponded to the importance of the message, he stuck out his Adam's apple.

"The fact is that from tomorrow your husband is the head of the department!" He blurted out, breathless and waiting for the impression the news would make.

"That's how it is! Well, aren't you a shuffler!" Malika put the plate in the sink and wiped her hands on her apron. "Should I hug you or will you do it yourself?"

"Of course I'll do it myself!" Sargel clasped his wife in his arms, pressed his lips to her cheek.

"Sar, dear, let's not disturb Karatai…"

"How would I 'disturb' him? Is it bad news?!"

"I'm not talking about that. I wanted to say, let's not talk about Bagila with him," Malika passionately kissed

Sargel. "Well, think about it, it's all nonsense. Why spoil the holiday in our house..."

Sargel's face, rosy from the kiss, faded again.

"You always spoil the mood."

"Well, excuse me," she again reached out to him with her lips, and then with her whole body. "We decided to go to the sea in the summer with Bagila. I think she'll be able to clear her head there. Find us two tickets to the Crimea. You're a doctor of science after all, head of the department."

Sargel moved to the window and looked out into the street, as if he saw the seashore there and on it his wife and Bagila in bathing suits, in close proximity to unfamiliar men.

"Can't she just forget him here?"

"No!" Malika put all her ardour into this "no", sensing that the conversation might stall. "You are a smart person, and you understand well how difficult it is for a girl. She's having such a dangerous time, help her distract herself!"

Sargel, twisted in a bundle of the most unexpected thoughts, loomed over the kitchen. Finally, he stopped in front of his wife.

"Tomorrow. Tomorrow, I will answer you..."

Malika silently agreed and returned to the plates. She needed to think things through. It was going to be a fun night ahead, she wondered how many questions he will ask and how she will answer them so as not to alert someone like Sargel?

Having barely finished the exams, Bagila left with Malika to the sea. It was true heroism on Sargel's part. He was exhausted to the point of heartache, until permission was given. Only the presence of his niece next to Malika somehow calmed him.

After returning from the airport, Sargel immediately called Karatai.

"Thank you," Karatai expressed his gratitude. "I'm glad you're treating her with such paternal care."

"Do not mention it!" Sargel replied with deliberate disdain. "Our common duty is to think about procreation. Bagila is our blood, our descendant. We all live for the sake of children!"

"Not everyone thinks so..."

Sargel was glad that Karatai liked him again and laughed.

"By the way, about that conversation... It seems that she threw him out of her head. Now everything is fine, calm, cheerful. I think sea water will completely wash her off him," Sargel did not notice that this sounded ambiguous, but Karatai was stung by this phrase. "It will return, and it will be insipid again, as before, without bitterness and without sweetness..." Sargel was clearly carried away, he was very pleased with himself. The next moment his face twisted, as if he were choking. "What…? When? No, why?" Surprised, Sargel's tongue stuck to the sky. "No, I do not know. I haven't read. These days many writers get divorced... Yes, they are all good, unless you re-read them! What? So, the grader driver had time, what does he... What? Well, what about the doctor of humanities?! I have lectures, public affairs, eternal fuss in the department. Okay, okay, I'm sorry! Yes, let him be at least three times as good. At least people can live these days, thank god, not bad, why shouldn't he write well?! We don't lie down either! Will have to read through. I once had it in my hands, but I can't understand a damn thing about him, he winds up and... Let him write, I don't feel sorry for him."

"Don't be offended, I'm just speaking the say way I usually do," Karatai laughed, feeling that he had hooked Sargel well.

"You're right, this is a smart position," Sargel climbed to score points, "We must also respect the enemy. Yes, what an enemy he is, he can simply become the cause of various rumours here and there, and you don't know how I always have to fight against gossip. Actually, I can't stand the writer's brethren... They are all womanisers and drunkards! This man is married, has two children, he is criticised every day in the newspapers, but he too…! Well, they say he drinks bitter."

"Hey Sarga, you don't understand me! I'm not talking about wanting to see him as my daughter's husband.

I'm talking about Madiev just as a writer, and I don't care what he does in his free time. Okay, enough about him! Listen, Sargel, why are you sitting in this dusty city? While they are gone, take the children and come to us. Stay for a bit..."

"God, I wish I could get out. Try to come over..."

After finishing the conversation, Sargel breathed a sigh of relief and went out to the balcony to freshen up. The sun had long since set, but the bluish evening light still flickered over the city. Sargel looked at the alley under the balcony and tensed, something familiar seemed to him in the figure looming near the entrance.

"Hey Serbota? Hey, you?!"

Serbota froze, caught off guard, then twitched and ran, crouching, around the corner. Sargel shrugged his shoulders in bewilderment and thought he had made a fool of himself.

Returning to the apartment, Sargel put his hands behind his back and began pacing the rooms. Everything was in order, cleanliness, neatness. Unbeknownst to himself, he found himself in Bagila's room in front of a photograph of his deceased wife and children. Sargel stopped in front of her, dropped his arms along his body. His eyes suddenly filled with sand... He did not immediately understand what kind of feeling squeezed his heart so prickly, because he forgot when it had last visited him. His eyes felt better, but hot lines appeared on his cheeks... What was that? God, is this loneliness? He's alone, that's why he always feels bad. And the children…? How could he forget about his sons?!

And on this day, dawn began far in the mountains, marking the peaks of Alatau with a white line.

After dinner, Jasyn slept for an hour and sat down at his desk. He had been writing all night and only now stood up and opened the window. Cool, damp air rushed into the room. Jasyn shuddered. His head was pounding unbearably, he sat all night without moving, he smoked a lot. The whole world was waiting for the sunrise with bated breath. The dense crowns of elms and poplars, hanging right above the window, have not yet awakened from their sweet predawn dream. Singing birds fluttered in the calm foliage.

How many times did he meet sunrises like this, but they never looked alike. "Dawns are like people, each of them has its own disposition, character…" thought Jasyn.

He returned to the desk, which stood some distance from the window. A heavy smell of stale tobacco smoke hit his nose. There was a pounding in his temples again. He sank heavily into his chair, bent over what had written during the night.

Just two and a half pages! And this was from eight in the evening until five in the morning. Two and a half pages of clean, worked out text in which not a single word has been crossed out. He hated text with blots and did not understand how you can possibly edit your own work. No, he was categorically against such work. "Pure art is not born twice," he believed. "A work of art cannot contain individual words; it is not a wall of bricks. Talent and thought are given to the writer so that he immediately finds what he is looking for. If you have to correct yourself in your mind, fiddling with words on paper - that is not creativity, but handicraft." Colleagues attacked Jasyn from all sides about his: "It turns out that only you create, and everyone else writes? But what about Pushkin, Tolstoy, Dostoevsky?! Do you think they are all artisans?!"

"Man is not a deity," answered Jasyn. "I don't bow to meat and bone. All in all, I think in my own way. Do I have the right to write neatly right away?!"

Jasyn read the two and a half pages again. He thought, worried, despaired and hoped for a talented engineer, scientist, who would propose to turn the desert into the river to irrigate the land, and suddenly found himself in a dead end. Jasyn liked the text. The door quietly opened, and his father appeared in the opening, wearing a white shirt and white underpants.

"Well," he said belligerently. "Sitting from morning to morning again? Are you trying to get into another fight?"

"Hey, buddy, close the door, will you?" said Jasyn, putting on a stern look whilst looking up and down his father's appearance. "What kind of kindergarten did you run away from?"

"Look at you, cheeks sunken, eyes like a hole in a well, you can't breathe in this room, it's like the hole of a stinking marmot. Why bother, it'll be all the same, the newspapers will pounce like wasps. Why are you torturing yourself?"

Jasyn laughed out loud.

"You go, buddy, go. The most you can do is choose a last name. Me and the pseudonym will fulfil the role of the father."

"Who is this pseudonym?"

"He's also something like a father, only prodigal. They are useful when someone is embarrassed by their real name."

Pushing the old man away from the door, his mother entered the room with a bowl.

"Oh, looks like Sophia Loren is here as well?!"

"Drink this," his mother said softly.

"Otherwise, your intestines will stick to back of your spine," said the father.

"God's sake, stop talking and go to your room," the old woman angrily flashed her eyes at the old man. "You cackle at the light, like a hungry chicken! Come on, let's not bother him." And she literally dragged the old man along with her.

Jasyn took the bowl. It was millet drink flavoured with kurt. Neither hot nor cold. Just right for a quick drink. It wasn't prepared last night. It was made today; took at least an hour at most. It turns out that his mother also does not sleep for him! He looked at his watch. Already six. In an hour, his wife and son will get up.

Jasyn closed the window, put out the table lamp and already moved into the bedroom, deciding to take an hour's nap, but then the phone squealed like panicked pig, the buzzer of which was set to the minimum. Jasyn looked at the phone in surprise and picked up the receiver.

"I'm listening," he said so quietly that no one could hear him.

On the other end of the wire, a woman literally screamed:

"Jasyn, is that you?"

"Yes."

"Sorry it's so early, but it's already dawn. For us it's..."

"Who is it?"

"It's me, Malika."

"Who?!"

"Malika. Remember?"

"Lord, are you from another other world? Malika from where?"

"From Yalta."

Jasyn was stunned.

"Hello! I'm listening..."

"We are here... We came here to rest..." Malika's voice broke off and reappeared a note higher. "Bagila is very ill. She is in the hospital. Yesterday…" Malika began to cry.

"How can I help?" It seemed to Jasyn that the sun was beginning to sink back behind the mountains.

"You… must come here. Be sure to come. You will understand everything here. I can't call for too long, it's hard for me…" Jasyn, after a little silence, said to her:

"Are you out of your mind? It's not like Yalta is Kaskelen! Do you know how long-" Jasyn cut himself off, he was lost for words, he didn't understand anything. "Besides, how will my arrival help?"

"Please, I'm asking you! At least for two or three days. I didn't mean to call you, but it happened. Will you come…? I'm running out of coins. I'm calling from a machine. Speak now!"

"It turns out, that I have to play the role of an ambulance, only one that's being called from Almaty?"

"You have a different role!" Malika screamed so angrily that Jasyn twitched in fear. "If it will become difficult getting a ticket, then there is a woman in the ninth box office of the agency, her name is Masha. Don't forget Masha! Refer her to me. Our building is next to the restaurant Priboy…"

The call ended, the phone squeaked and rustled like damp wood…

"That's crazy," Jasyn thought, freaking out. "They should call me for serious matters instead of stocking up on pennies! Yalta! When did they even manage to leave?

It looks like this was all her idea, that Malika!"

After their meeting at the hotel, Jasyn called Bagila twice. Her voice was cold, humiliatingly polite, Jasyn was offended and stopped calling. On reflection, he decided to pull himself together and try to get her out of his head, but as soon as he thought about it, a wound began to grow in his soul. He realised with horror that he could not forget Bagila, that she would live until the last minute in his callous heart, which did not know tenderness. He was not afraid that he would ruin the girl's life, this was not the main concern for him. He was afraid of one thing, that someday he would get used to her beauty, before which he bowed, and Bagila would become for him as insipid as his wife. Jasyn remembered a parable about a man who, having become engaged to the daughter of a saint, a rare beauty, was inflamed with passion for a woman with a crooked mouth and dull eyes five years later...

He thought about something in his office for a long time, then nevertheless went to the bedroom. Silently opened the door. His wife was sleeping, he entered quietly, but she still moved, looked at him through her eyelids swollen from sleep and turned over on her other side.

Jasyn took off his dressing gown, stood by the bed, watching his wife sleep, and lay down in their warm bed.

He arrived in Simferopol at noon. He rushed to Yalta on a taxi and easily found the Priboy restaurant and their building next to it.

A crystal evening grew thick over Crimea. Malika was not in the room. Everything was familiar to Jasyn here, he had been to Yalta several times. Literally last spring, he rested in the Writers' House of Creativity, and here he finished the first part of his story. In the spring, Yalta seemed deserted, but now the city looked like an anthill. There were no people dressed like Jasyn, he thought that it was simply indecent to walk around in a suit at this time of the year.

There was nowhere to stand on the shore, it was entirely filled with human bodies. The day was long over, and the people seem to have grown together with the sand. Vacationers swarm to the very bend of the cape.

He bought newspapers and sat on the edge of the bench. On the other side were three girls. They were in a great mood. Jasyn admired their tanned dense bodies from the side. They looked at him, dressed like he was crazy, and began to discuss the plan for the evening.

People walked endlessly past the bench. "How beautiful! Interesting," Jasyn thought. "It's not just a re-sort here in the summer. It's a festival of beautiful figures. A competition of stature and passion."

"Hey girls," said the one who was sitting closer to Jasyn. "I completely forgot! Last night I had a wonderful dream. The whole world has become as warm as Crimea, there is no winter at all. Everyone goes around only in bathing suits, and suddenly one person, can you imagine, one out of a thousand, appears in a suit, and instead of undressing, he walks like a white crow, even reads the newspapers! He's even proud to wear a tie. And what do you think? The police took him. There he was shown how to dress properly!"

The girls laughed. Jasyn realised that this whole "dream" was invented only for him, to hook him up. He was ready to respond to them but stopped himself.

The girls got back to work.

"Look around: do you see any police around here?"

They burst out laughing again. Jasyn knew this laugh – it was carefree, healthy, coming from complete idleness, a feeling of happiness and a desire to please someone, right now, immediately and to the very end.

"Yes, it's impossible to approach the educated, what are we compared to them, they know how to read! This unfortunate coast of Crimea! No matter how much it turns into an all-Union reading room!"

This time Jasyn could not stand it, he was offended and not overly politely said:

"And then the god, walking on the water, appeared to the maidens, like mermaids, and said: I leave you here, by the water, forever naked. From now on, you will please my angels and guess their dreams. Remember, if a person rides a bright horse in a dream, they will achieve a high rank, but if they sit next to the king and shakes his hand, they will rise in the service, and if they catch a fish in their dream, they will have a child. If naked people dream, they will soon go crazy... Explain to people the dreams of angels, and do not follow this covenant, my crucifixion awaits you in life ... "

Their laughter was cut short. The girls looked at him, Jasyn was sitting, still buried in the newspaper. One of them craned her neck.

"Did you read that in there?" She asked with child-like curiosity.

Jasyn was once again convinced of the female stupidity, grinned to himself, having folded the newspaper neatly, as if it was the most valuable thing, he got up from the bench, like a saint who had come from heaven, and majestically retired, noting with satisfaction that the girls had been blown away by the wind.

As soon as he knocked on the door, Malika ran out to meet him. Ignoring the people around them, she immediately hugged him.

"Finally! I've looked all over for you!" She burst into tears. "Couldn't you have come sooner?"

Jasyn felt uneasy from such a meeting.

"How are you?" Jasyn asked, rather rudely removing Malika's hands from his shoulders.

"A little better, but yesterday I was terribly scared, I thought that she might die." Malika began to cry again. "Bagila talks about you all the time. It was you... that hurt her so much. Why did you…? Do it…?"

Jasyn didn't know what to say.

"What's going on with her?" He asked when Malika thought to invite him into the room.

"We didn't know anything, but it turns out she has a bad heart. We decided to move away from you, but you see what happened..."

Crimea clearly benefited Malika. Her face was flushed and rounded. Her wrinkles disappeared, and the bruises under her eyes disappeared. She was prepared for Jasyn's arrival: her short hair was fashionably curled with a small comp. She wore a colourful chintz dress that was deliberately sewn tightly so that her figure was immediately visible. "Damn it," thought Jasyn. "She knows her charms well. How self-conscious can these women be, Bagila is in the hospital, and she couldn't forget to run to the barber. At the same time, she is a good person."

"Can I see her today?"

"I have a pass. If we can explain, they'll let both of us pass. Only... What if she sees you and becomes worse? Let me go in first..."

It was already dark when they approached the hospital, surrounded by cypresses. It was a completely different world, silence, deserted. Only the blows of the waves faintly reached the hospital building and the cheerful voice of the guide, who called out to the vacationers on the other side with a megaphone.

Realising that Jasyn had come from afar, the doctors allowed him to go into the ward. As they agreed, Malika entered first. She almost immediately returned for him and silently nodded in the direction of the ward.

Bagila was sat up on the pillows, the blanket pulled over her chest... She decided to be self-possessed, unresponsive, but when she saw Jasyn, she lost her breath, her heart pounded in a haunted way. Noticing this unexpected excitement, the nurse sitting by the bed was seriously frightened. Here, no one knew what this guy had to do with the patient, but having discovered such a change in behaviour, the lady whispered to Jasyn: "No more than two minutes, you hear!"

Jasyn approached her, Bagila tried to smile, but when he sat on the edge of the bed and took her hand, her eyes filled with tears.

And Jasyn's heart sank. He stared with fixed eyes at the thinned girlish finger lying limply in his palms. Their quiet warmth was slowly transferred to him, and Jasyn became agitated, he heard his troubled heart. He thought that after the stupid meeting in the hotel, they were seeing each other like this for the first time in a while, that their separation was impossibly stupid and senseless. Why did they not see each other for so long. He kissed her guiltily on her hot, dry lips. The nurse watched with surprise as Jasyn kissed the patient in front of everyone, and she only closed her eyes and smiled softly. The lady could bet that the girl got better.

"This time your lips smell like medicine," Jasyn smiled softly.

Bagila nodded.

"First time in a hotel, second time in a hospital. Will there be a third..."

"Don't talk so much." Jasyn shook his head. "These days people are even afraid of colds. Don't be like them."

"I'm sorry that everything turned out like this," she felt awkward in front of Jasyn. "Lika thought up of all this. She's a great inventor... When are you flying back home?"

"When you get better."

"Oh, I might be lying here for a while, and you have a lot of things to do. And then there is your family..."

"Stop talking about that," Jasyn frowned, "And finally stop speaking so formally"

Bagila looked at him carefully.

"You have become affectionate. Am I wrong?"

"God forbid!" Jasyn answered, although in his heart he admitted that it was so. "I'd be old by now if I did."

Bagila laughed, there was some truth in this joke. The nurse, Malika and Jasyn himself willingly joined her laughter. They also talked about some little things, Jasyn tried to joke. Finally, the nurse remembered why she was in the room and began to rush them.

"Fly back tomorrow," Bagila managed to say with ease. "I'm asking from the bottom of my heart."

"Am I going to stop you from getting sick properly if I stay here?"

"Yes. In this state, it is difficult for me to see you.

Besides... my father is arriving in two days. The doctors informed him. If he sees you so suddenly... Well, you understand!"

"Of course, I understand…" Jasyn pursed his lips. He started thinking, "Her father will see me and nothing good will come of it. I've lived for this, yet there is nothing I can say!" He smiled bitterly. "I'm not allowed to love anymore. I can do everything else; I have the right... These damned rules, nothing ever happens on time. Where was she when I was single when everything was ahead of me? Is it really necessary to lose something equally precious in order to find something else? Why is that?"

He fervently squeezed Bagila's hand.

"Come on, when you arrive in Almaty, let's go and walk in the park?"

"Are you going to get some ice cream?" She smiled ironically.

"I don't know, I kind of want some..." He shrugged.

"Well first. you need to be in Almaty."

The next day he came to say goodbye to Bagila.

"Goodbye, Sur. Remember, the first thing I will do when you arrive in Almaty is drag you to the park!"

"Oh, what a hero!"

"Don't laugh. I'll be offended!"

"Looks like we switched roles! Okay, I've already agreed with you," she turned to the window so that he would not see her tears.

Malik rushed to calm Bagila, but her attempt to caress the girl backfired, Bagila wept limply. Malika looked at Jasyn, in her eyes he suddenly read a malicious condemnation and shuddered shiveringly.

"How are the Almaty newspapers? Did they criticise you?" Bagila asked through the tears, saving Jasyn and Malika.

"Not yet, but there is still time, they will not miss their chance." He tried to joke, but Bagila did not accept this tone, Jasyn added quickly: "I will come again, for sure. I'll bring it to you myself. In a week."

Bagila shook her head. "No need. I'll come to you myself."

No more words were needed. He felt that none of them, even the smartest ones, would be more important than Bagila's last phrase.

He silently got up and walked towards the exit. At that moment, the door opened, and Karatai and Turgat entered the ward together with the chief physician. Karatai slashed his gaze, like a whip, on Jasyn's face. The head physician spoke up.

"It's bad that you didn't notice the illness in time," he said, looking past Karatai. "Of course, it's not a disaster, modern medicine copes with this diagnosis. To be honest we didn't have to disturb you, but we had to inform you..."

Karatai, listening to the doctor, approached his daughter, pressed his lips to her forehead.

"It's all my fault, I'm sorry," he whispered. "How could I not have noticed! As the father I should have known." His voice trembled. Karatai turned away, took out a handkerchief, darted furtively into it, and wiped his eyes. After greeting Bagila and Malika, Turgat decided, since he also came from afar, that shaking hands would not be enough, and kissed Bagila on the forehead. Exactly in the place where Jasyn kissed her.

"I stuck to my father like a burdock," Bagila was angry with herself for not having time to move away from this person. "My father probably doesn't know why Turgat followed him..."

Once Bagila received a letter from Turgat. He wrote that he had built a house of eight rooms, that these rooms were well furnished and that only the most expensive, golden thing was missing - Bagila. He also wrote that he was respected in the region, that Karatai Isaevich didn't have a soul inside him, but that Turgat himself still cared for him.

Turgat reported that he plays sports every day, how he trains his calves and works them every day... In a year, his calves would be able to press 150 kilograms, but, in his opinion, he will master this weight without much difficulty.

Bagila involuntarily chuckled and looked at the door. Jasyn was not there. She laid her head on the pillow and sighed wearily.

He walked along the crowded avenue, seeing nothing but the biting glance of Karatai, which hit him like knife.

"He looked at me with contempt. He was not surprised that in distant Crimea, in the hospital room of his daughter, there was an unfamiliar Kazakh," thought Jasyn. "He recognised me, yes, he knows me. Damn it, how his pupils trembled…! And he, it seems, is not a bad person. What did he say to his daughter? 'It's all my fault, I'm sorry. How could I not have noticed! As the father I should have known.' He really is tormented…"

Suddenly he remembered his own children. He did not know why, but before his eyes, they appeared lying in beds, in a hospital ward. Their eyes were full of tears. And all of his relatives stood in a crowd in the ward.

"Their father will not come," they said. "He will never come. He will not shed a tear and say: 'It's all my fault.'"

Jasyn felt unwell, the blood pounded painfully in his temples. He was lost, he ended up on the edge of the city. He went out again to the street leading to the centre. He wandered without any meaning or purpose.

When the sun hit the sea horizon and the water turned golden, he went to the bus station.

It was fifteen minutes before the bus left. The passengers were already seated. There were no tickets. As Jasyn approached, appearing suddenly out of nowhere, Malika ran up and stood at the entrance of the 'Ikarus' bus.

"Oh, thank god, where did you go? I almost lost my mind!" She blurted out, barely catching her breath. "The bus is about to leave."

"So what, if I don't take this one, then there is always the next one. The plane is at twelve o'clock."

"What a calm person you are! Fine, fly how you want to fly. There will be no more buses after this, and you'll die of boredom on the bus-tram."

Jasyn noted of Malika's efficiency with pleasure. In Yalta, where you won't find a plane ticket if you need to fly urgently during such hot summer days, she managed to get one. "Without such people, life is not life," thought Jasyn. And no one appreciates her. Besides, she is pretty. Still, a woman should be beautiful! As if afraid that she would read his thoughts, Jasyn averted his eyes from Malika.

"After you left, Bagila felt bad, but now it's easier... You see, they completely forgot about you!" she said in a playful tone.

They laughed as they looked at each other.

"I think you must be the instigator of this whole mess?"

"Yes I am!" Malika coquettishly adjusted her already well-fitting straw hat.

"A straw hat suits you," Jasyn necessarily complimented. "When are the guests leaving?"

"Ah, yes," Malika said, clapping Jasyn on the shoulder. "Karatai asked about you. I was scared to death. I thought he would tear my head off, but he didn't even say a word against it. I don't think he hates you that much. But this Turgat! Oh boy!" She put her hands on her head. "He is planning to take Bagila to Almaty himself. Karatai is flying back tomorrow, but this one is staying here..."

Jasyn looked straight at her. And Malika did not lower her eyes. A blush appeared on her cheeks and began to quickly spread over her face. Realising this, she fluttered her eyelashes.

"When we return, will you be in Almaty?" Malika asked pointedly.

"What do mean 'when we return?' I said I'm going back before that..."

"No need. That guy is going with us. He doesn't like you. In general, he does not like writers at all."

Jasyn lit a cigarette, looked distantly as the smoke dissipated.

"I know."

"How? Did Bagila tell you?!" Malika was surprised with his immediacy.

"No, I can see it myself, I guessed from his eyes. For such people, ambition replaces intelligence. This is visible to the naked eye."

Malika listened with undisguised admiration. The bus hummed warningly.

"I'll walk you to the airport," Malika said languidly.

"Are you out of your mind? To go all the way to

Simferopol? Besides, you don't have a ticket."

"Remember, Malika is a great specialist when it comes to tickets. I can even get a ticket for yesterday's plane!" She laughed.

"No. Stay close to Bagila. Perhaps Karatai is looking for you."

"I told him..."

"What exactly did you say that you decided to come and see me off?!"

"Nothing you need to worry about. What's wrong with telling him, let him know..." He just shook his head.

"You're a tough nut to crack," he said, emphasising the 'you' specifically.

Malika lowered her eyes modestly.

Jasyn climbed the first step and immediately looked back: Malika's eyelashes were trembling, holding back tears. Jasyn, wanting to cheer her up, said to her with a laugh:

"So, you haven't been able to come up with a nickname for me for several years now, have you?"

Malika, like a child admitting their guilt, spread her hands...

He watched her until the bus rounded a rocky hill...

Again and again, he thought about Bagila, that now they would not strive to forget each other, about the words of the father to his daughter, coming from his heart, about Malika's recent tears. Why was that woman crying? He will never know this. Somehow, the fatigue that had accumulated over the past weeks immediately flooded in. In a light, half-sleep on the road, his wife and two children again stood before his eyes. God, why is he seeing them in the hospital room? Why are people's faces so pale…? And the children? And they too… What are his relatives doing here? They seem to be saying… Yes, he clearly hears: "Their father will not come. He will never come. He will not slip through and say: I'm sorry, it's all my fault."

1979

TURMOIL

DULAT ISSABEKOV

TURMOIL